A Farmer's Daughter

A Meadow Romance

Sian Sibbons

Chapter One

Flemsbury, Gloucestershire 1854.

The crowing of a rooster announced the start of a new day in the Mayer household. Rubbing her sleepy blue eyes, Emily emerged from under the woollen blanket draped over the bed and stretched her slim arms to help the blood move through her frozen veins. Seconds later, she padded barefoot across the rough oak planks to the tiny window carved into the two foot cobbed walls. Dawn was breaking over the fields of Gloucestershire and the spring sky was a palette of red and purple streaks creating a stunning moving landscape. Whatever the time of year, the vivid image was an early morning tonic to Emily who saw wonder in all weather.

Beneath the wooden floor, a creaking door followed by the clanking of pots could be heard. There was no time to enjoy the familiar sight that greeted her most mornings; the working day had already begun. After washing her face in a basin filled with cold water, she put on her black milking dress, slipped on woven straw shoes, and climbed down the curved staircase, ready to start the new day.

Downstairs the farmhouse comprised three equal-sized rooms, two of which were used only for working. One, built onto the rear of the property and accessible only from the outside, was used as a dairy. The other working room was for washing, spinning and weaving. It was the kitchen that was very much the heart and soul of the farmhouse. With its small windows and huge fireplace taking up most of one wall, it was always warm and welcoming regardless of the season. On either side of the fireplace were two high-backed chairs used more by the ginger cat, Missy, than the family. Mr and Mrs Mayer and their son and daughter preferred to sit around the large oak table where together they ate, talked, laughed and cried.

As soon as Emily stepped onto the grey flagstone floor, she noticed that all four dining chairs were empty. That wasn't a surprise as it was rare for the whole family to have breakfast together lately. Since Pete had finished a few weeks earlier, they needed to do the extra work in the fields which meant working from dawn to dusk most days. Employing even one labourer was a luxury they could no longer afford since the railway station opened in the village. Cheap travel to factory towns and cities meant that the unskilled could demand more wages to stay local. And John Mayer's small holding made barely enough to keep the family in food, let alone a young man with small children of his own. So, having worked there for ten years, Pete had taken his services to Birmingham, leaving the family to manage the farm between them. It was going to be far from easy.

The only other person in the kitchen, Emily's mother, Mara, was pouring boiling water into a large teapot. She was annoyed that her husband had not allowed himself and Sam even a hot drink before starting the long day. The man could be reckless with his health. At forty-five, John Mayer was still strong and fit, but his bones ached more every day. The lines on his still handsome face betrayed the concern he felt for the farm's future. Both father and son needed to give every ounce of muscle to cultivating the fields; but as tenant farmers, so much was out of their control. Would there be anything left for Sam to take over?

Leaving the pot to stand, she took the hunk of bread that had been toasting over the hearth and spread it with dripping before wrapping it in paper. Then she smiled at her daughter.

'Take this to your pa and brother, luv. I don't want them pulling that rake on empty stomachs.'

'It's Duke and Duchess what do all the pulling, Ma,' Emily said, rolling her eyes.

'Don't be funny, my girl. Those horses would turn a snook at that dripping and you know it well. Go on! Yours will be waiting for you by the time you get back.'

Emily took the parcel of food and, ignoring her mother's command to put on a coat, ran out into the brisk morning. It was the best way to shake off the sleepiness. She loved the dawn air flowing over her bare skin like she was a creature of nature, a deer or a badger, rushing through the countryside while humans slept. All the time she trod carefully to spare the dew-soaked flowers which had yet to unfurl their petals. But the invigorating feeling ended the moment she saw a dark shape moving ahead of her.

As she got closer a ray of fresh sunshine lit up her brother's porcelain face and the siblings waved to each other. Holding out a long slender arm, Sam walked over to his sister eager for the sustenance she was carrying. Even in the dimness, his light blond locks and cornflower blue eyes managed to reflect the meagre light in the sky. With his chiselled features and high cheekbones, he could almost be Emily's identical twin if it were not for his stronger and more mature jawline. A year older than Emily, he was still growing, caught between youth and maturity. But five years after leaving school at fifteen, he regarded himself as a working man.

'You are starting earlier every morning,' Emily said, looking around for her father.

'There'll be no point in going to bed soon,' he said, ripping off half the bread and shovelling it in his mouth. 'This tastes good. No tea?'

'I couldn't carry it all,' she said, frowning at the dripping covering her brother's square chin. 'I'll come back with some after feeding the hens.' She felt a strong arm on her shoulder and turned to see her father smiling at her. 'Morning, Pa.' She smiled brightly and kissed his rough cheek.

'Morning, my girl,' said the older and more weathered version of Sam. 'We've another glorious day ahead of us. What are you doing out here at this time? Don't tell me,' he said with a playful roll of the eyes, 'You heard the lad's stomach crying. Well, he's not a baby nor am I.'

Emily laughed as she handed over her father's breakfast but inside she worried as much as her mother did. Lately, her father seemed just that bit shorter than when he used to tower over her, and his shoulders a little less broad than when they once carried her. Instead, his shoulders stooped slightly especially when he thought nobody was watching. Emily expelled the glum thought from her head as she watched her father return to the wooden plough he'd left. At least he was doing the work he loved rather than down some old mine or inside a factory. The Mayers were country folk through and through and Emily was no different. Although she'd never be able to push the plough like a man, her work in the dairy brought in a substantial amount of income which the family could not do without.

Back in the kitchen, as promised, Mara had already poured two cups of strong tea and cut some more thick slices of bread. In contrast to her slim, angular husband and children, she was petite but curvaceous with a round face and dark hair. She would often joke about how she found Sam and Emily under cabbage leaves even though both closely resembled their father. While Emily scraped raspberry jam over a smaller piece, her long hair was being brushed and tied up by her mother. Mara always insisted that Emily never lifted the wavy locks high enough which allowed wispy strands to hang down. *Nobody wants a golden thread in their breakfast*, she would say each time her daughter screeched in pain.

'I already fed the hens, and you don't need to worry about the men,' Mara said. 'I'll take them their tea. You get started on the animals.'

So, after swallowing the last of her tea, Emily made her way into the nearby field to collect two cows she then led to the milking shed. A few minutes later, with her white apron and cap on, she began working the first of two daily milking shifts. Those were not all her duties, not by far. Between the milking, she would join her mother in skimming and churning to produce butter and cheese. It was heavy work but also called for skill and experience. Despite being only nineteen Emily possessed both. She positioned herself on the three-legged stool and started to milk.

***

James Murdoch had forgotten to pull the curtains closed before falling into bed and now he had to cover his dark eyes to shield them from the sun streaming in through the large bedroom window. Six chimes came from the grandfather clock outside his bedroom door and, realizing he had only gone to bed a few hours earlier, he slumped back between the sheets. As the minutes ticked by, James's tiredness began to lift leaving him to suffer his hangover in full. Realizing he was unlikely to get more sleep while feeling so rotten, he dragged himself out of bed and staggered over to the wash basin where he sank his face into the stagnant water hoping it would wash away his headache. It did not.

Since returning from university, James had been out almost every night, whether to a party, a gentleman's club, or an alehouse, and the fast living was starting to take its toll. Douglas was forever saying they should make the most of being young and wealthy as there would be no fun after marriage, and he was probably right. Yet the way James was feeling at that moment, he doubted he would live long enough to find a wife. There were plenty of female admirers in Oxford, but he certainly was not ready to commit himself to one yet.

Hearing footsteps pass by his bedroom door, James was reminded that it would not matter what his feelings were about marriage because his father would likely make the decision for him. No, his life was not his own to lead so Douglas was definitely right. He should live life to the fullest while he still could. He took off the crumpled evening suit he had slept in, changed into his nightwear and once again let his head hit the pillow.

***

The new day was showing its colours in the crop field. What had begun as a tiny glow on the horizon was now casting an array of reds and oranges across a gradually lightening sky. The visual feast was accompanied by a serenade of birdsong that filled the air with sweet melodies. John and Sam Mayer, however, were deaf and blind to those wonders of nature having experienced them so many times over the years. Starting in one corner of the field, John led the horses and rake while Sam followed collecting the cut wheat. With a long hard day ahead of them they spoke little preserving all of their energy for the laborious work. Although few words passed between them, each one's thoughts occasionally strayed to his companion. That morning, Sam's head was filled with frustration as he watched his father dragging the horses pulling the rake, three weary creatures pushing their bodies to the limit. His father was a proud and dedicated farmer determined to bring out the best of the land on which several generations of the family had lived and worked. But Sam imagined that the lives of their ancestors were easier than their own.

Seasoned farmer Hans Meier and his family had emigrated from Hamburg during the eighteenth century preferring the relative stability of English life. Anglicising the family name, he quickly made a reputation for himself as a skilled and reliable cultivator of land and became the most important farmer for miles around. But those were better times when there were more fields to grow the crops that men were employed to pick. In those days the Meiers were not merely farmers but also employers of many labourers and providers of much of the village wealth. That was before trains. Some farms benefited hugely from the wider markets that the advent of the railway brought. But that had come at the cost of scarring the countryside with hundreds of miles of steel tracks. Squire Charles Murdoch was one of the landowners all too willing to sell his fields for that purpose resulting in the Mayers' farm being reduced to little more than five acres.

John Mayer was a conservative man with a narrow outlook on life. Preferring to travel by horse and cart, he saw no advantages in the new mode of transport. Further, to his son's annoyance, he refused to ask the squire to invest in more modern farming methods. Unlike his father, Sam was excited about the changes he'd heard about and could not wait to experience the inventions that had broadened every horizon. He would be willing to leave the backwater that was Flemsbury and start a new life in the city where the hard work was now done by steam instead of people. But his father's world was his family and farm and he could not see beyond them, not for himself nor his son onto whom he expected to pass the farm. Sam had not yet the courage to disappoint him.

***

It was still a beautiful day when Emily took her late-afternoon break after both milkings. Now changed out of the unforgiving dark work clothes, she cherished the feel of the light blue cotton dress against her fair skin. As she strolled through the meadow close to the farmhouse the butterflies danced around still flowers lounging under a pale blue cloudless sky. Freed from the white cotton dairy cap, her natural blonde curls flowed freely over her delicate shoulders to her small waist. With her long slim legs and lean body, she had not inherited her mother's curves but no one would mistake her for anything other than a young woman. At that moment, however, Emily was alone with no one watching her, at least from the human world.

Her eyes, reflecting the colour of the sky, followed the funny Red Admiral fluttering its tiny wings around her head and tickling her forehead. Then a bee approached and the butterfly flew away clearing the view of the yellow-speckled greenness ahead. Nearing her favoured spot, Emily kicked off her shoes and ran lithely towards the elm tree where she liked to sit. The sensation of the soft grass against the soles of her feet was like heaven to her, and she expressed her joy through a succession of cartwheels to extend the feeling to her palms. With each rotation, pieces of food dropped from her pockets but that was fine because they were not for her. Energy spent, she sat down and leaned back on her hands to enjoy the warm sun rays on her face while she waited for her friend to appear.

Ten minutes passed without any activity so Emily sat up and squinted in the sun looking for movement. Her rose-petal cheeks changed to white as her watering eyes met a blurred figure staring in her direction. Though in the distance, fifty yards or more away, and just an outline, she could tell from the height and build that it was a man, a tall man. His agile movement showed he was young too, though maybe older than her by a couple of years. The figure battled with the clumps of overgrown meadow grass to get more into the open flat green field of pretty bluebells and primroses to move closer to the young lady he could see in front of him. As he approached, he lifted the hat from his head and waved it in a show of friendliness. His thick hair seemed as black as the tailcoat he was wearing as did his eyes.

'Hello,' he called out. His voice was raised but gentle as if not wanting to startle her. 'I noticed you sitting here as I was passing. Are you a member of the farmhouse family?'

Emily had never heard a voice like his, the words gliding from his mouth like syrup from a spoon: soft, regular and somehow graceful. There were no lengthened vowels or rhotic 'r's like her own. His was not a local accent yet he did not appear to be a stranger to the area as he knew about her home. Puzzled, she nervously gave a half smile and replied, 'Yes. Who are you?'

'James Murdoch. I live at the manor house or at least my father does along with a few helpers. You will not have seen me around much as I have been away for several years.' Then he grinned, his dark eyes flashing with what could only be described as mischief. 'Now you have something on me.'

'What do you mean?' Emily replied with a confused expression.

'Well, you know several things about me whereas I know very little about you. Tell me your name.'

'Emily Mayer,' she said quietly.

'So, Emily Mayer, what are you doing sitting in my father's meadow?'

'Your father's?' Emily gasped in fear. 'I don't understand. I thought this was common land and that nobody owned it.'

'All land is owned by someone or something, Miss Mayer. Did your father not teach you that? I am making the assumption that your father is the local farmer.'

'Forgive me,' she said, her voice quaking and dread flowing through her mind. 'It won't happen again. I'll go now.' She stood up, grabbed her shoes and started to run back to the farmhouse but heard his voice calling her.

'Where are you going? Come back!'

Frightened at the firm tone she stopped dead in her tracks and slowly looked around at him. Was he going to drag her to the magistrate's court and demand a fine be imposed? Her father would be so cross with her. But the young man was smiling.

'Stay here by all means. I did not mean for you to leave besides you seem so content here as though you are part of the meadow.'

Emily hesitated before replying, 'But maybe your father would mind me being here unlawfully. He is, as you say, the owner of this land.'

'Unlawfully?' the young man said, laughing. 'Well, I shall own it one day and my law says that you are as welcome here as any other bluebird.'

'A bluebird.' That's a strange thing to say, she thought. 'There are no bluebirds here.'

'That's what you remind me of.' James took a step closer to Emily and held his hands towards her. 'Bluebirds are graceful creatures attracted to meadows, like larks but far more beautiful. And with your pretty dress, you are a bluebird.'

If I am a bluebird, she thought, what are you? A predator? But she no longer felt nervous and was beginning to warm to his words. It was a rare experience to be flattered by a young man as grand as him, and she was in no hurry for it to end. Also, her curiosity about the dark stranger was growing. 'Why have you been away for so long?' she asked him, suddenly feeling more confident in his presence.

His glinting eyes betrayed amusement at the question. 'Do not worry. It is all very innocent. I have been at Pembroke for the past three years studying Classics even though my father wanted me to do Law which I know, is just as dull.'

'If you say so,' she answered while brushing stalks of high grass with her palms. 'What's Classics?'

'It is the study of the ancient civilisations of Rome and Greece which involves learning hundreds of useless words and phrases just to show you are cleverer than those who have not.'

'What kind of words?'

'Latin and Greek words. Both languages are barely used anymore, except in places like Pembroke, of course.'

'My grandmother was from Carmarthen but she only spoke Welsh.'

He frowned then threw his head back laughing. 'Pembroke College. It is part of Oxford University. You are funny, Emily Mayer.'

But Emily didn't laugh. 'How am I supposed to know about your university? I've never even been to school, except on Sundays and they didn't teach me about colleges in Oxford. You only know because you go there.'

Hearing the scorn in Emily's voice, James held his hands up as if in surrender. 'Forgive me for laughing but it is not at you but rather at myself. Pembroke is one of the lesser-known colleges of Oxbridge which my friends at Magdalene and Christ Church rib me about all the time.'

'Well, I haven't heard of those either,' she said, pushing her aquiline nose into the air. 'What use would ancient languages be to me in a dairy? Though I suppose the cows would understand them as much as any other living creature.'

'Is that what you do, Emily? I can picture you sitting on a tiny three-legged stool underneath a huge brown cow called Daisy.'

Feeling that she was being belittled, Emily snapped, 'And if I didn't, you wouldn't get milk in your tea, now would you?'

'I do not take milk with my tea, actually, but I appreciate your point and am grateful to you all the same.'

With a shrug of the shoulders and a slight smile, Emily signalled that her mock offence had passed. However, she decided not to ask any more inquisitive questions which might inflate his ego further. Besides, it was approaching the time when she should be getting back to the farm. But just as she was about to open her mouth, he spoke first.

'May I sit with you for a while? My legs are crying out for a rest.'

There was no answer to his request as Emily was still standing. But he continued.

'Please,' he said, gesturing for her to sit back on the flattened grass.

Emily looked at him with suspicion again unsure whether he was to be trusted. But how could she trust a complete stranger, even if he claimed to be the squire's son? And a feeling inside made her want to trust him. So she placed herself a few more yards away just to make a point as the ten yards that separated them would be futile if an escape was needed. Somehow she sensed it wouldn't be necessary.

'Oh, how I have missed this,' he said, looking around him. 'There is nothing Man can make which compares to the wonder of a meadow.'

'Don't they have meadows in Oxford?' The question was genuine.

'No doubt there are fields and meadows in every county but I never stray far beyond the college grounds hence my lily-white skin. It has its own wonders, such as the River Thames, but that is always littered with boats and barges.'

A relaxed silence fell over them for the first time as if they were not two people who had met only minutes earlier. A female blackbird appeared in the space between them and dropped the wriggling mass it had been holding in its dark yellow beak. Both watched mesmerised as the bird intermittently pecked at the poor worm between staring into space. Emily had seen the bird many times before regularly bringing it bread and cheese left over from meal times. She knew it felt safe in her presence even though her father told her blackbirds were some of the most stupid birds and didn't know what was good for them. Not stupid, she thought, just trusting. The sound of melodic birdsong came from a nearby tree and the blackbird flew up to join her mate disrupting the interlude in conversation.

'Why do you come here alone?' he asked her. 'Do you not have a sister or brother to keep you company?'

'I have a brother, but he is busy in the field with my father. I don't have any sisters. My parents married late in life and say they were blessed to have my brother and me though we all know another boy would have been far more use to them.'

'But then who would milk the cows?' he said with a grin.

'There are plenty of men that milk cows,' she replied. 'And the churning is not an easy job.'

'I am sure it is most difficult. But you cannot spend all your time with cows. Do you have friends?'

'Not really. There's no time for friends and most of the girls my age are already in service so I don't get to see them anymore.'

'You say they are already in service. Does that mean you intend to join them in such work?'

'No. I am needed on the farm,' she said proudly, 'so service is not an option for me.'

'That is a heavy burden for you. Why does your father not employ labourers to help him?'

'There is not enough work to pay another man's wages. We manage between the four of us.'

'And I can see that you are happy even without company.'

'I have all the company I need in my family.'

'Unfortunately, families do not last forever.'

'What do you mean?'

'Well, your brother for instance. He is certain to marry soon and most likely leave to start a new life.'

'No, because he wants to take the farm over one day. He will always be here,' Emily insisted, despite having some doubts. She'd noticed the faraway look in her brother's eyes of late but had not the courage to ask him his thoughts. 'What about you? Do you have brothers and sisters?'

He shook his head. 'Not anymore. There was a sister, Juliette, but she died when she was three. Then two years ago, my older brother, Edward was killed while posted in India. So, while I am away, there is only my father living in that grand old house, and a few servants, of course, but he does not talk to them.'

'What about your mother?'

'Last year, she went to stay with her sister in Turkey, caught diphtheria and died over there.' His eyes glazed over slightly as he took a moment to wallow in his private thoughts.

As Emily listened to the words coming from his pale lips, she wondered how such smooth unblemished skin could cover all the brutal heartache he'd endured throughout his short life. But she'd heard about the stiff upper lip of the gentry classes, how they saw it their duty to keep going regardless of personal hardship. It was a world away from her own family who often shared tears of joy, grief and sadness.

Suddenly, James got to his feet and brushed down his trousers, saying, 'I should go now. Thank you for your company. I must return to Oxford to finish my exams. Perhaps if you are here again next Friday, we can continue our conversation.' He gave a slight bow before turning around.

Emily watched as he walked away, his figure getting smaller and more blurred with every step. Just as he was about to disappear completely, he stopped for a few seconds before continuing to walk until he faded into nothingness.

Chapter Two

Emily lay in bed the following Friday with her eyes open before the cockerel sounded. With no memory of waking up, she wondered if she'd had any sleep at all. Despite that, she felt wide awake and when the alarm finally called, she leapt out of bed with an extra spring in her step. After spending more time than usual washing herself, she slipped into her work dress and rushed downstairs to find both her parents and Sam already seated at the table. From upstairs she'd heard them having a long discussion which continued until Emily opened the door separating the kitchen from the stone staircase.

'Good morning, dear,' Mara said quickly. 'Sit yourself down. The tea's piping hot.'

‘What were you talking about?’ Emily asked, catching the glances exchanged between her parents and brother.

‘Nothing of interest to you, sweetheart,’ her father replied. ‘Your mother was going through the accounts with me, that’s all.’

‘And how are the accounts, Sam?’ Emily tried not to show her irritation at still being regarded as a child. If her brother was old enough to know, so was she.

‘We are getting by as always,’ her mother said quickly. ‘Now, first things first.’ She stood up and pointed to her vacated chair.

Emily sensed an air of gloom despite the glow coming from the hearth. ‘I hope you aren’t keeping anything from me. I’m nineteen so that makes me an adult like you.’ She cried out as her mother yanked at her hair without any warning. Assuming that was the end of the conversation, Emily turned to eating her breakfast despite the strange curdling in her stomach.

But Sam had decided otherwise. ‘She does have a right to know,’ he said, looking up at his mother rolling her eyes. His father nodded.

As she chewed on the scrap of toast in her mouth, a feeling of dread swept over Emily despite her earlier words. She listened as her father shared their news with her.

'The lease on this farm is up soon and the word around the village is Mr Murdoch is likely to not renew it for a long period like the family have always been used to. He might only renew it for another year.'

Emily realised that she was not as grown-up as Sam because, after hearing her father's words, she was little the wiser. What was a lease? Swallowing her pride, she asked and remained quiet while Sam gave a brief account of the agreements signed between generations of the two families.

'So there you have it, sister. For over a hundred years our family's livelihood has depended on the whim of a man whose only care is for the money he can make. The latest man does not even care for money, it seems.'

'Now don't you go badmouthing his name around the village, son, or he's likely to refuse to sign anything at all,' John said sharply.

Still confused, Emily continued with her questions. 'I don't understand why he wouldn't sign it for longer. You say this has never been a problem before. Besides, is a year lease so bad?'

Mara swallowed a mouthful of tea before giving her opinion. 'It suggests that he is tired of the farm. His father, Robert Murdoch, was a good man. He gave us twenty years and invested much of his money in the land. Charles

Murdoch has never shown the same interest in the farm allowing it to go to wrack and ruin under his ownership. He's more interested in using the land for hunting than growing wheat.'

'Well, there's still the dairy,' Emily said. 'That doesn't need much land apart from a hen coop and a piece of grass for the cows to graze on.'

'That won't keep us going for long,' Sam said. 'Without the land for crops, there won't be enough to live on.'

For the first time during the conversation, the pessimism in the air took hold of Emily and she had to fight back the tears. 'But we've always lived here. He can't make us leave.'

John shook his head. 'That's not how it works. He owns the land and if he doesn't want to sign another lease, nobody can force him.'

'But people need wheat and vegetables and milk. They can't live on dead foxes.'

Such remarks were childish and pointless and Emily fell silent after speaking them as she could not trust herself to say something worthwhile about the situation. It did not matter as the men were on their feet and heading for the door. Mara disappeared upstairs to collect the laundry leaving Emily to sip her tea while absorbing what her family had told her. She'd never considered a time when the farmhouse would not be there for her even when Sam took it over — or if he didn't. It was so unfair that their entire livelihood could be turned upside down because one man wanted more land to hunt on. What kind of a horrid man was Charles Murdoch?

***

Emily looked towards the older grass at the far end of the meadow. From where she was sitting it was easy to see any movement in the near distance and there was no sign of him yet. Only the blackbird kept Emily company but was too busy pecking at the dry ground to notice her. She lay back on the soft green carpet and reached to the nearest daisy gently brushing its petals with the tips of her fingers. Staring up into the deep blue sky, she looked for faces in the speckles of white clouds imagining that they were also looking down on her. In one cloud was the figure of a horse leaping over a low snowy hedge, another showed the smiling face of an old man. She wanted to believe that the sky was the resting place of those who had passed on from their previous life. It would be a wonderful way to spend eternity.

With the gentle breeze, the clouds gradually broke up and formed new images, releasing the sun from its hiding place. The sudden dazzling light caused Emily to close her watering eyes and enjoy the warm rays on her skin. After a few minutes, the narrow shafts of light between her flickering eyelids disappeared, and a cool sensation washed over her face. She opened her eyes to see him gazing down at her, his damp hair hanging down freely like a black stallion's mane.

'Hello, Emily. I am sorry if I kept you waiting,' he said, without retreating an inch.

'What do you mean?' she said, shuffling backwards before sitting up and wiping the moisture from her lips. 'I was not waiting for you. I'm here as I normally am.'

He swayed slightly and, after steadying himself, replied, 'Sorry again for being so presumptuous. May I sit with you?'

Emily nodded. She did not know what presumptuous meant but preferred to keep her ignorance to herself this time.

'I seem to have frightened Madame Blackbird away,' he said, looking around him. 'Perhaps she does not trust me as she does you.'

'She'll be back soon,' Emily said, spinning a daisy between her fingers. It was unlike her to pick the wildflowers, but somehow she felt less exposed with something in her hand as though a daisy could act as a barrier.

'I suspect you know much of the wildlife in this meadow since you come here every day. And they know you also.'

She smiled despite not knowing if it was meant as a compliment. 'I hope so. It is their home, after all, and I am only visiting.'

'You mean trespassing, do you not?' he said with a smirk.

Not responding to his teasing question, Emily moved on to a different topic. 'Do you hunt?'

With exaggeration, he jerked his head to demonstrate his surprise at the question. 'That is an odd thing to ask me. Of course, I hunt occasionally though not, I must add, blackbirds.'

Emily took time over her reply. 'I heard that your father wants to use the farmland for hunting so will not sign another lease for the farm. That would mean we'd have to find somewhere else to live.' The words hadn't come out as she had rehearsed inside her head but it was too late to retrieve them. She hadn't wanted the family to sound so dependent on the acts of others.

James shook his head. 'I had no idea that he was planning to do that.'

Emily shrugged her shoulders pretending not to care so much. 'How could you not know? You and your father have only each other to talk to.'

'It is quite simple. It was up to my brother to take an interest in the estate being that he was the heir. As the younger brother, I was meant to make my living away from the manor. That is why I have been away for so long. There was no need for me to be here. When Edward died everything changed.'

To hear him talk about his family home in such a matter-of-fact way shocked Emily. He clearly had no idea how other people lived. But perhaps she could be the one to show him. 'Does that mean you will stay here?'

'Well, my father is not dead yet so I am not bound to remain here for the time being.' He was silent for a while as if he was thinking.

'But where else do you have to go?' Emily said.

'Listen, I shall speak to my father about the lease. He is not such a bad old thing so I am sure he will reconsider his decision.'

Emily was so excited to hear those words that she wanted to run home and tell her parents there and then but didn't dare upset him in case he changed his mind. Also, she did not know if he had any say in the matter. 'That's so kind of you. Do you think he'll agree? It is such a worry for us.'

'Do not worry, Emily. I shall make him agree.'

Deciding there was little more she could do to reassure herself, she returned to her unanswered question. 'If you are not staying here, where will you live?'

'It is not that I am going to live anywhere,' he replied. 'But I am too young to settle in one place. There is a whole world to explore first.'

To Emily, James was not so young but she thought better than to mention it. Instead, she focussed on his fantastic plans. 'The whole world is much too big for one person to explore.'

'Perhaps, but England is much too small to live one's whole life in. I have already spent some time in Rome and Alexandria but big cities are full of tourists. I want to experience different ways of life.'

'Where would you like to go?' Emily asked. Once again she was not sure of his meaning.

'Possibly Calcutta where my brother was. I have heard an Englishman can live as a king in India.'

Emily imagined that India must be full of people like her family working hard while a privileged few lived in large houses and spent their time dancing and hunting. Again, a world away from her own.

James continued to ponder aloud over the next few years of his life. 'But I think I might pass some time in America first. My uncle has a plantation in St Kitts which is a little paradise and not too far from Virginia. Then there is the Far East. This summer, I shall be spoilt for choice.'

Most of those places meant nothing to Emily, and her mind drifted away from James' musings. Gazing over his shoulder she could see the blackbird looking back at her as if knowing her thoughts. Suddenly, realising there was only silence, she refocused her eyes and saw that he was staring at her.

'What is it?' she asked. 'Why are you looking at me like that?'

His lips turned upwards but in a smile rather than a grin. 'Am I being a bore?'

Slightly embarrassed that he knew she hadn't been listening, she apologised. 'No. I'm sorry but so much of what you say is strange to me. You live in another world which I understand very little about. Sometimes it is difficult to keep up with what you are saying.'

'Then I shall stop talking and listen instead. Emily Mayer, where do you want to go? What are your dreams?'

As if to serenade her words, the male blackbird appeared and started to sing though her answer was far from romantic. 'My dream is to stay here forever', she said, without hesitating. 'Why would I want to be anywhere else in the world?'

He smiled. 'Why does that not surprise me? You are as much a part of this meadow as the daisies around us and the grass in your hair.'

Instinctively, Emily's hand brushed against her head and pulled a blade of dried grass from it. She blushed but he laughed causing her to smile shyly. That emotional reciprocity created an air of intensity that was tangible to both. Even the blackbird fell silent. For the second time, Emily got to her feet. James followed her lead.

They walked back through the overgrown grass together until reaching the wooden stile at the end of the family farm. The conversation was of a far less personal nature than earlier centring on the trees and flowers they passed. Emily could name each one from only its touch or scent while James was content to listen and learn. He held out his hand to aid her onto the step but she nimbly climbed over without help and stood facing him on the other side.

'May I join you again on Monday?' he asked.

'If you wish,' she replied with a coyness she could not hide. Feeling the heat rising in her cheeks, she turned and ran towards the farmhouse and wondered what he would be doing until Monday.

***

James arrived back at Manston Manor just as a carriage left the forecourt. He recognised the grand barouche as belonging to the Harding family who resided in the next county. It was too late for an arrival so James assumed that he'd missed the visit and wondered if Letitia Harding was in that departing carriage. If so, his father would be furious.

Slipping through the servants' entrance, he bumped into a surprised maid.

'Pardon me, sir,' she said, her face now crimson.

'Ah, Tess. I am going out tonight so shall be taking a bath at seven o'clock,' James said, without looking at the young person he was addressing.

'Seven o'clock, sir!' she replied too quickly.

'Yes, Tess. Does that time not suit you?'

'Forgive me, sir. I didn't hear you properly the first time,' Tess lied. 'I'll have it ready as you wish, sir.'

James did not reply because he was already creeping up the stairs. After opening the door to his room he marched over to the two large casement windows and pulled across the heavy emerald and gold embraided drapes to shut out the daylight. Rather than struggle with the tightly made bedclothes, he lay down on a red velvet chaise longue to rest. He needed to get some sleep before evening if he was going to keep up with Douglas. That man could have a barrel of beer head start and still drink him under the table. To make things worse, Douglas never seemed to suffer the next day in the way most men did, and James suffered more than most.

James' head was swimming when he'd met that girl in the meadow and she was lucky he wasn't sick over her. He must have looked and smelt a state. He certainly felt one. Perhaps that was why she was keen to keep her distance. But not far enough to prevent him from capturing her image. Waves of fair hair around cornflower eyes emerged through the darkness behind his closed eyes. She certainly was a beauty. There was something more to her than a young pretty face or the suppleness of her slim body. He smiled thinking of his first sight of her, with her legs in the air like a circus acrobat. Or like a child. Yet she was not so young as all that. Eighteen maybe, but certainly innocent - and naïve. He should probably leave her alone.

Chapter Three

Sam Mayer looked around nervously as he and the rest of the family sat down on the last vacant pew. They were later than usual after waiting for Sam to finish washing and dressing. When he'd eventually appeared from his room wearing a brand-new necktie with his perfectly ironed morning coat, Emily burst into a fit of giggles, resulting in him turning to go back upstairs. But a stern voice called him back.

'Come on, lad,' John Mayer had said. 'There's no more time for you to look at yourself.'

Sam had finally followed them out of the farmhouse, his cheeks burning with shame at Emily's reaction and his father's words. He knew their teasing was goodhearted but the butterflies in his stomach were already making him queasy. As they had walked into the church he couldn't bring himself to move his eyes from Emily's back. Now seated, his adrenalin returned and he scoured the pews like a periscope searching for enemy ships. Yet, the person he was looking for was far from his foe. The congregation was at full capacity allowing virtually no spaces to sit or peer through. At last, he caught sight of a familiar blue bonnet on the other side of the aisle and, satisfied she was present, turned around to face the vicar. Sam had cast eyes on her many times before and was familiar with every freckle on her pretty nose. He wondered if the nerves that overcame him every time they met would eventually decrease. He hoped they wouldn't

It wasn't a bonnet that held Emily's attention but an emerald velvet hat worn by a lady in the front pew. Unfamiliar faces were rare amongst the churchgoers except on the second Sunday of each month when a visiting canon gave the service drawing many from surrounding villages. Emily couldn't take her eyes off the chestnut-haired woman, not because of her rather flamboyant hat but the man she was sitting next to. It was James Murdoch. For a while, Emily tried to convince herself they were as much strangers to one another as she was to the portly gentlemen whose legs were pressed against her own. Everyone had to sit close to another person whether they knew them or not because the church was so crowded that not even a tiny space could be left between them. But towards the end of the very long sermon, the woman leant into James and whispered into his ear. It was like a dagger to Emily's heart. Despite hating herself, she continued to watch for any interaction between the man and woman in the front pew her thoughts alternating between anger, resentment and misery. She was angry at James Murdoch for bringing himself to her attention when she had known virtually nothing of him. Her resentment was towards the unknown woman in the velvet hat whose clear pedigree qualified her to sit with the squire's son. But the intensity of neither emotion came close to that of the misery that seeped through her body as she tried to focus on The Lord's Prayer.

Once the tray had passed around the pews, all left the church in single file ready to acknowledge and give thanks to the visiting canon. The amount of time given to each person depended largely on their status in the parish. Last in line but first in rank was Squire Charles Murdoch who also wore the grandest frock coat and tallest hat. He was preceded by his son James whose hair and clothes were rather dishevelled for church. Both Murdochs exchanged a good few words with the canon. In contrast, the Mayer family members merely nodded or shook his hand neither noticing nor caring about their standing in the canon's eyes – except Emily. Mara, in particular, would have had little time for such displays of privilege being a former Methodist preacher. In her mind, all souls were equal regardless of wealth or other earthly possessions.

Emily had been one of the first out of the church and waited impatiently while Sam and her parents chatted with some other parishioners. Hurry up, she thought, desperately not wanting to be there when James emerged with the mysterious woman in the expensive hat. Suddenly, she heard a gentle voice behind her and turned around to see Lilly Bexley walking towards her.

'Hello, Emily,' Lilly said, in almost a whisper. 'What are you doing by yourself? Oh, I do like your bonnet.'

'Thanks, Lilly. Yours is pretty too. I'm waiting for the rest of my family. Have you seen Sam yet? He was looking for you the whole time we were inside.'

Lilly blushed. 'It was so full in there I couldn't see anyone at all, except for the back of the fat lady sitting in front of me. I could give you a full description of every piece of fruit in her awful hat.'

'Hush,' Emily whispered, glancing around quickly for the woman Lilly had so rudely described. Thankfully there was nobody near enough to hear the insults but she noticed Sam who was already walking towards them. As if sensing his approach, Lilly turned around to greet him.

'Hello, Lilly,' he said with his eyes fixed on hers. 'Are you in a hurry to go home? If you like, I can walk you back to your village.'

Lilly gave a smile which lit up her whole face. 'Yes, that would be nice. It is a shame to waste such a pleasant morning. Good to see you again, Emily. I hope your parents stop talking soon.'

Emily watched the young couple as they started the two-hour walk which should take only one. She knew Sam was deeply in love with Lilly and it was easy to understand why. With auburn curls, eyes of almond shape and colour, red lips and a button nose, she was as close to a perfect doll as any human could be. With her glossy hair neatly tucked into a pretty bonnet, nails shaped and clean, and her frock somehow creaseless, she always looked and smelt immaculate. In contrast, Emily's hair didn't like a hat, its wayward strands always slipping through any pins and clips. She didn't worry too much about cleaning and filing her nails as she knew they would get dirty or broken again. And, apart from when she went to church, no one from outside the family saw her, and the cows and chickens didn't seem to care much about her clothes.

Once again standing alone, she gave a sideways glance at the church door only to see James stepping away from the canon. Although there was a respectable distance between them, the woman in the velvet hat was still at his side and was now able to display the fullness of her white bell skirt and fur-trimmed mantelet. Emily stared enviously at her ridiculously tiny waist and wondered how she could walk, talk and breathe while looking that elegant. On her other side was a man of a similar age with whom she was deep in conversation. James gradually walked on with his head down as if lost in thought and oblivious to his surroundings. Emily's eyes followed him as he moved forward and she thought he looked unwell. His skin was white with a yellow hue and his dark fringe stuck to his forehead. He kept walking until reaching the largest and grandest of the waiting carriages. Once there, he turned his full attention back to his two companions who instantly involved him in their conversation. Emily held her breath as she waited to see who would enter the carriage praying it would not be James. To her relief, only the woman climbed into the vehicle leaving the two men to continue their journey on foot. Turning her attention back to the carriage, she observed how elaborately ornamental it was compared to others which were far more practical in their design — just like that woman.

***

It was a long walk to the neighbouring village of Corbury but Sam and Lilly were in no hurry to reach their destination. Walking arm in arm along the narrow road that seemed to wind itself in circles, the young couple talked of their hopes and dreams. Of the two of them, Lilly was the most certain about where she would be in a year or two. Having worked as a maid at the Fortesque house since she was nine, she had seen and heard enough to know that there was an entirely different world outside their tiny area. Although a mere scullery maid when she'd started, her current position was Lady's Maid which allowed her to brush shoulders with the young ladies of the house. As she plaited and adorned their hair with ribbons, the daughters would tell her of the latest ball or opera, the giant parks with lakes and deer, stone palaces built many centuries ago alongside the fabulous Crystal Palace made entirely of glass and iron. In contrast to the bleak, boring and bland countryside, London was a mixture of old and new, rich and poor, dark and light. And Lilly could not wait to be part of it.

Sam viewed his world through a much narrower lens and his focus was merely on the woman he loved. Wherever Lilly wanted to go, he would take her. Until they met, he had no thoughts of living anywhere other than Flemsbury and like his father and forefathers, expected to be a farmer. The reason for having that attitude he blamed on his relatively sheltered upbringing in a family that barely left the village beyond going to market. Occasionally his mother would tell them of the many places she'd travelled to as a young woman preaching to anyone who would listen. She would always end her accounts with the one where she met her future husband and father of her children. *And my long journey was at an end*, she would say with great pride. In that sense, so was Sam's. Since setting eyes on Lilly his eyes stopped straying towards pretty girls because none of them could compare to her. As if to reassure himself, he bent down and kissed her on her cheek.

'You are naughty, Sam. What if someone was passing?' she said playfully.

'Then I'm sure they would be most jealous of us,' he replied with a grin. 'But if you would rather privacy, there is an old barn up ahead. It is just the place for a rest.'

Sure enough, after another ten minutes or so a small building came into their sights. When Lilly saw the ramshackle straw roof and warped walls she thought she'd tease Sam.

'I couldn't possibly go in there,' she said.

'Whyever not?' Sam asked, trying not to show his disappointment.

'Well, for one, this dress is made from pure silk and I could not bear for it to be scagged by rusty nails. Secondly, I would hate to get straw in my hair.'

'Oh, Lilly. I would never do anything to upset you. We shall walk on.'

Lilly burst into laughter. 'Don't be silly. I'm playing games with you.'

Relief in his eyes, Sam picked up a screaming Lilly in his arms and carried her into the rundown barn. Once inside, he lay her down gently on some straw and kissed her passionately. He did not have to ask her if it was safe as their trust in each other was complete. They made love as they did when any chance came their way. Neither could wait for the time when they were not so dependent on chance giving them an opportunity.

When it came time for them to brush themselves down and proceed with the journey, Lilly brought up the situation with Sam's family and how he needed to persuade his father to employ a labourer once again to soften the blow of his only son leaving the farm.

'There are plenty of local young men who would gladly do the job for free if they could move in with your Emily,' she said.

'Don't be daft, Lil. Do you think our father will let any man live in the house? The last one was when me and Em were young enough to share a room.'

'Don't you mean you and your father won't let anyone?' Lilly teased. 'You will have to give up being the big brother when she gets married.'

'If our Em does get herself a husband, it won't be some labourer who can't even demand a wage.'

'True,' Lilly said. 'Maybe we should take her with us. I bet she's never set foot out of Flemsbury.'

'Nor does she want to. She's more like our father than he is like himself. No, Emily will never leave that farmhouse.'

'She is so lovely I cannot understand how she hasn't already been whisked off her feet.'

'Oh, several have tried,' Sam replied, 'but she's never been interested in them. As I said, Em will end up an old maid churning milk and weaving hats.'

Lilly shook her head. 'Then it would be a good thing if the farm closed, and she would be forced to leave. Do you think we should ask her to join us in London?'

Sam did not reply. The security of his parents' future was more than enough to concern him. Emily would have to take care of herself.

***

A silent Emily walked home behind her parents who were arguing over their absent son. John Mayer was not happy with Sam's growing relationship with Lilly who he feared would take him away from the farm.

'We have to hope he hasn't lost his mind over the girl or he'll be giving up his whole future. She's got the bright city lights in her eyes,' he said, 'and won't be content living in a country village much longer. Working in that grand house has gone to her head. She forgets she's a mere servant girl and that's all she's likely to be in a city too. And our Sam's likely to follow her wherever she goes without a job of his own. Let's hope she finds another lad to take her first.'

His wife, though agreeing about Lilly, didn't share her husband's wish for her to leave Sam. She knew her son well enough to see the change in him from the moment he met Lilly. He took greater pride in his appearance, laughed more, and ate less. She recognised in him the certainty that he had met the woman he wanted to spend the rest of his life with. 'Let us see what happens. We don't know the future. Lilly might change her mind but if she goes, and if, our Sam goes too, we shall find someone to replace him on the farm.'

'But to leave behind what his family have held for so many years, Mara, it's not right. And what would he end up doing in Bristol or London? There is no good job for the skilled man. It's all factory work or loading ships.'

'But she'll be on a wage too and some of those textile jobs are very well paid. What would she do if they married? She'd have to give up her position in the Fortesque household and there is nothing else around here for her.'

'She could let our Sam take care of her, that's what. If she's so fond of him, she should let him make the decisions.'

'So, the girl is strongminded. She isn't going to change who she is, and Sam wouldn't want her to.'

Emily had to bite her tongue not to join the conversation as she knew her opinion would not make a difference. Both parents were set in their ways and wouldn't change their views. Her mother had no fear of the unknown. Born in a family of itinerant methodists, she'd spent her young life travelling through the county without a thought for the places left behind. That was until she'd fallen in love and was willing to give up the life she'd known for a man she hardly knew. In contrast, the man who would become her husband was traditional and set in his ways. John Mayer rarely went outside of the village and, having little interest in what lay beyond, could not understand those who did. Though Emily admired her mother's adventurous spirit, she shared her father's views on life. To leave a place there should be a better one waiting for you - and how could anywhere be better than Flemsbury?

When they arrived back at the farmhouse, they found a letter pinned to the front door which John warily removed. As he read the letter his mouth turned increasingly downwards. It was obvious that the content was not welcome.

'It's from Murdoch. He's not going to extend the lease beyond this year. That only gives us another six months. Well, we'll see about that. I'm going to speak to Jim Hawkins tomorrow. He'll know what rights we've got.' Without saying another word, he refolded the letter and placed it in his pocket.

Emily and her mother exchanged glances but didn't speak. They all entered the kitchen and sat down at the table where they remained for a long time staring at the cold teapot in the centre. No one got up to light the hearth or start the dinner as each one was busy with their private thoughts. Mara was worried about her husband as she knew life would continue with or without the farm. If necessary, they would leave and start up somewhere again. They had some of their own money invested in the farm and that would help them until they found other work. But she knew how much John loved the farm and it would break his heart to leave. Inside his head, John was cursing

Charles Murdoch who he knew cared nothing for the people living and working on his land. It boiled his blood that a man with so few Christian values could be given the most time by the canon.

Emily was also angry at the Murdochs but more at James who had promised to speak to his father about the lease. It was so cruel to give her hope if he knew it would make no difference. Or had he just forgotten? She thought he probably had yet this made her angrier still. Thank goodness she hadn't told her parents because they would have been filled with hope too. But that would have meant telling them about her spending time alone with James in the meadow. Even her mother might not have approved of that.

By the time Sam returned, the fire was lit and dinner was being dished out. Judging by the constant grin on his face, his journey with Lilly had been pleasurable. Catching her husband's eye, Mara shook her head and the contents of the letter remained between the three who had been present when it was opened. Somehow it seemed the wrong time to tell Sam.

Chapter Four

Speckles of water coated Emily's cheeks as she walked under the dark sky to the chicken coop. There was no dawn glow on the horizon, only heavy grey clouds foreshadowing a stormy morning. There would be little shelter in the meadow but the weather was not a problem for her; rain, wind or snow had never put her off before ... before. It used to be her special place shared only with the wildlife, and she cherished the sight of every leaf and blade of grass existing through all the elements. But that was before he intruded into that world. Lately, her eyes searched not for the blackbird or the squirrel but for him striding through the long grass dressed in his black coat, satin waistcoat and plaid trousers. With his tousled dark hair and moody expression, he could be a painter or poet searching for spiritual influence from nature, yet he only appeared to search for her. Why? Probably for little more than his own amusement with no regard for her feelings. She would not go to the meadow that day.

***

Mara was preparing a stew in the afternoon with some of the ham left over from the previous evening meal. Buying the meat had been an extravagance so it would have to last them a few days, but John and Sam worked a long and hard day so needed a wholesome meal to keep their strength up even if it meant giving herself and Emily meagre portions. With her thin yet strong arms, she placed the pot on the stove and wiped the grease and vegetable juice from the table ready to start on the accounts. It was a task she always left until the dairy work was finished as she needed to concentrate without thinking about the next thing she had to do.

The first concern was the rent on the farmhouse. Even if the lease was not to be extended, they still had to pay rent for the time they remained. In the past, they had been able to pay at least part of that in kind. However, the last few years had seen output drop to such a level that it was more economical to sell all of their farm produce in the market at a higher price than what it was worth as rent. Besides, the less business the family had with Charles Murdoch, the better.

A gust of wind blew the papers off the table as Emily opened the door and entered the kitchen.

'What are you doing here at this hour, luv?' Mara said, hoping her frustration wasn't showing through her large eyes.

Emily picked up the scattered papers and returned them to the table. 'The weather is so bad I decided to stay in and help you.'

Mara smiled. 'Well, I'm not sure there's anything more to be done. Why don't you see if your brother needs a hand.'

'I already did and he said he's fine.'

Sensing her daughter wanted to talk, Mara put down the bill she'd just picked up. 'Well, there's a kettle that could do with boiling and a teapot waiting to be filled.'

When mother and daughter were sitting opposite each other, mug of tea in hands, they spent some time discussing the well-being of the individual farm animals. Eventually, the subject of the farmhouse came around.

'Have you heard anything about the lease?' Emily asked.

'Now don't you go worrying yourself over that, my girl. It's for me and your father to sort out.'

'I live here too. Of course, it affects me. Our family has been here for so long that I can't imagine ever leaving.'

'Listen, luv, a lot can happen in six months. Jim Hawkins thinks we've got a good case for staying here beyond six months. He said we need at least a year to prepare and is willing to speak on our behalf.'

'What good is another few months? We'll still be homeless. It's so unfair. Wait! Perhaps a mistake had been made and the letter was not meant for us. Or he was drunk and didn't know what he was doing. I'm sure he will soon change his mind.'

Mara shook her head more in anger at Charles Murdoch than in disagreement with Emily. It broke her heart to think of her daughter being thrown out of the house in which she'd been born and lived for her whole life. Emily was a young woman but in many ways still a child, dependent on her parents for a place to live and seemingly no desire to leave the nest. It would have been better if she'd spent time in service to gain some independence but she insisted that she was needed in the dairy. They would have managed well enough without her and possibly renting out her room while she was away.

Two years earlier, Mrs Barker had told them about a live-in position at Stanworth Hall, which, being only two miles away, seemed perfect. Emily had agreed to an interview and was all set to go when she became unwell and had to take to her bed. Mara and John knew their daughter well enough to recognise the reason behind her illness. After talking it over, they decided to tell Emily she was still needed on the farm and to forget about the position at Stanworth Hall. They felt justified in their decision when Emily was soon well and as happy and carefree as ever. However, now Mara had her regrets and could not hide her worries behind a relaxed expression.

'What's the matter, Ma? You look upset. Are things so bad?'

Forcing a smile, Mara switched her attention back to the present. 'Nothing is ever that bad, luv, and the world spins around so fast, problems are soon behind us. In a few years, you'll be married with children of your own to fuss over.'

Emily was surprised to hear her mother's words as she rarely talked about any of her family leaving the farmhouse. Unless she got married, which she thought unlikely, Emily assumed that she would remain living at the farmhouse milking until the proverbial cows came home. Even if she were to marry, very few young people could afford their own property so usually remained with one set of parents. She knew her mother well enough to know there was little use challenging her however there was one fact that she could not help but point out.

'But you were near thirty by the time you got married. If I wait that long, I will be living here for another ten years or so, won't I?'

'That was different because I was too busy travelling around with the church. I never intended to wed anyone until I met your father. You will meet someone long before that and he will take good care of you.'

'If you say so,' Emily replied, without enthusiasm or conviction. She had never before given much thought to marriage believing that few men could provide her with as much contentment as she already had in her life. Relating to possible marriage, Emily had set herself high standards which were not related to financial security or even good looks, but mutual love. 'Ma, tell me again how you and pa met.'

Mara's face lit up as the distant memory came back to her and, as her dark blue eyes turned misty under the long thick eyelashes, she described the moment her life changed. 'We'd come to the next village to preach and, when it was my turn to speak, I noticed a young man, tall with white-blond hair, standing amongst the people surrounding us. I could barely concentrate on my lines with the way he kept staring at me, but I knew he wasn't listening to a word I was saying. When I stopped speaking, he smiled. That was when my whole outlook on life changed. He asked if he could meet me the following day and he brought a ring with him. It was only made of straw but it was the most romantic thing in the world.'

'So, you gave up your whole way of life for a man you'd just met. That was brave.'

'It didn't feel brave. I suppose I should have been concerned that I was abandoning my calling but it was all so magical I believed we were meant to meet that day.'

'Did Grandpa try to stop you, or did he like Pa too?'

'Grandpa didn't like anyone but knew I was lost to the group so he gave us his blessing. By then your father was already a farmer with a few men working under him. He was a good catch for a plain old maid.'

Emily tried to picture her mother twenty years earlier without the greys in her dark hair or lines around her pale lips. Her father, a few years younger, had seen something beyond the frumpy clothes and uncoloured face. 'What was it like to fall in love at first sight?'

'Better than all the riches in the world. The feeling that you have met the man who is meant to be with you. It does not happen to many.'

'Do you think Sam and Lilly are meant to be together?'

Mara paused before answering. 'Maybe. He certainly believes that.'

'But you are worried about them, aren't you?'

'No. I'm worried about your father. He wants Sam to follow in his footsteps and thinks Lilly will steal him away.'

'Like father stole you away from Grandpa,'

'Yes.' Mara laughed. 'And that worked out well enough. Soon after, we were blessed with Sam, and then you of course.' Her eyes lifted to the ceiling at the memories before her attention returned to Emily. 'But you will have that too, my love. Just be patient. You are still a girl.'

'That is just as well, as no suitors are around this area.'

'There are plenty but you don't see them because you're too busy looking at the birds in the trees. The village fair is coming up soon and there will be lots of young men searching for a pretty girl like you.'

Emily squirmed at the thought of being on show for locals to judge her worthiness as a bride. She already knew most of the men who were going to be there as few outsiders came to the fair. There would be Danny Smith for one. He would ask her out for sure because he asked out all the single girls in the village and every time they would say no. At the other extreme were the Carter brothers who had been out with half the girls in the village before leaving them for the next girl. So, there would be few surprises at the fair. Even the travelling entertainers and tradesmen tended to be the same people year after year. Yes, she was fussy, perhaps too fussy, but she so wanted to experience instant love just like her mother, and Sam. For one absurd moment, she thought she had, but that was when her head was up in the clouds. It hadn't taken long for her to fall back down to earth, and it had been a painful landing which she was scared to repeat.

***

Charles Murdoch was standing at the library window, his usual place during the daytime. Like his son, he was tall and handsome but that was where the similarities ended. With his olive skin, hazel eyes and light brown hair, it was clear to everyone around him that his youngest son had not taken much after his father. Some might even have wondered if James really belonged to him if it were not for one shared characteristic — impetuosity.

Through the large Georgian panes, he watched the small group of young men and women strolling along the perfectly manicured lawn. Two women were walking on either side of his son, James, who was seemingly enjoying the attention of both equally. However, Charles was focussing on one, Arabella Fortesque, not because she was the prettier of the two, but because she came from an older family. The Fortesques were members of the aristocracy, albeit quite minor, and a marriage between her and James would raise the Murdoch name and reputation. Since James returned from university, Arabella had visited the house several times though never once by herself. She was always in the company of Douglas who was himself a better marriage prospect for her. He knew James didn't feel ready to marry yet but Charles was not prepared to wait until he did. Since Edward died, the survival of the family depended on James and it was now his duty to produce an heir. The family had not had the greatest fortune when it came to securing the line, therefore, the sooner James wed, the more heirs would likely be produced.

Charles continued watching as Arabella dropped back to walk with Douglas leaving the second young woman in front with James. Letitia Harding was from a family who had made their wealth through the changes in industry at the end of the last century. They had far more money in the bank than many aristocrats like the Fortesques. Land and position in society would always be more important than wealth but the latter may have to do. And Letitia was a handsome young woman who had a healthy build – buxom with childbearing hips. In contrast, Annabella oozed charm and possessed a delicate beauty that men would fight a duel over. With James' good looks and intelligence what a magnificent child they might produce.

Eventually, the small group walked out of his view and his attention turned to a third woman, but one who had not moved in years. From above the marble mantlepiece, the near-black eyes of Catherine Murdoch stared back at her widowed husband as they had done since first painted twenty years earlier. The image captured a moment in the honeymoon period of their life together when Catherine was young and healthy, and they were still in love.

He'd met her while spending a year studying in Madrid. She had milky skin and raven hair, a blend of the far-reaching Habsburg dynasty of which she was a distant member. With Dutch and Spanish parentage, she was a living doll made from china, black silk and blue blood. It had been a whirlwind romance leading to Catherine travelling to England as his wife. As a young man, Charles was an impetuous romantic and people around him assumed his action in haste could lead only to repentance at leisure. However, the couple enjoyed several years of great happiness. Although initially devastated by the secret wedding, his parents found her charming and accepted her into the family with open arms. Whether or not her lineage helped soften the blow was by the by to Charles as he believed they would have loved her regardless. He never stopped loving her, even when she left him.

A respectful knock on the door brought Charles back to the present and he returned to his favoured spot before responding.

'Enter!'

James walked into the study and gave a deferential nod to his father. 'Good afternoon, father. You wanted to speak with me.'

'Yes, James,' Charles replied, staring through the window rather than at his son. 'I wish to enquire about your plans for the next few months. Are you intending on remaining here?'

These were the meetings James always dreaded. His father saw him not as a young man but as an heir to his estate. He had no interest in his last remaining son's ambitions and wishes. Rather, James was regarded as the next rung in the ladder of prosperity. Everything was different when Edward was still alive. His brother had been the focus of his parents' wishes and James was allowed almost a free rein to find his own way through life. But now there was no escape. He knew that it was his duty to continue the family line in the most successful way possible, and he would do so, but he wasn't ready yet. He turned to his father's question. 'For a short while, father.

'What are your plans?' Charles said curtly, looking at James at last.

'Umm, I have not decided yet. Perhaps I could do some travelling.'

Charles turned back to face the window as if not wanting to see his son's reaction to what he was about to say. 'You are twenty-two this year. Is that correct?'

It was a ridiculous question but James answered all the same. 'Yes, that is correct.'

'I think it is about time you considered settling down. You are still a young man but not too young to marry. Have you given much thought to this?'

'Not yet, father. I wish to see some of the world, first.'

'Oh, you can do that. I only ask that you are engaged to be married before going.'

'Before going? But that is soon. I am not even courting anyone right now.'

'Miss Harding is a fine-looking woman and she comes from a good family. I was watching her through the window. She is very fond of you.'

'Letitia!' James had to swallow hard to stop himself laughing out loud. 'We are hardly friends, father. Douglas knows her far more than I do.'

'Then perhaps you should make an effort to know her more. I could invite Mr and Mrs Harding for dinner later this week.'

'Look, Letitia is good company, but I really cannot imagine her as a wife.'

'Imagination has nothing to do with it. What about Miss Fortesque?'

James paused.

'Ah!' Charles continued. 'You find her far more pleasing, I see.'

'Miss Fortesque is a very charming lady but I feel it is far too soon to consider her in such a way.'

'Perhaps you should begin to. I am giving you the chance to make your own choice, within reason of course, but I shall not wait long.'

After spending only a few minutes in the room, James was dismissed, leaving his father alone with his thoughts. He knew his son all too well. James was as impulsive as he had been, and it was only a matter of time before he made some rash decision that would irreparably affect his future. Charles was determined not to allow him that time.

When James returned to his friends in the sitting room, Douglas immediately got to his feet and led him back outside the door. He knew his friend well enough to recognise the troubled eyes.

'Has something happened?' Douglas said quietly.

James shook his head. 'No, nothing important. It is just father trying to control my life.'

'So, he wants you to take over the estate sooner than you thought?'

'Not even that. He wants me to get married as soon as possible. I don't even have anyone to ask yet.'

Douglas could not stop himself from laughing at a predicament he knew he would be in one day. 'Who is it to be?'

'It is not a joking matter, Dougie. He was evaluating the girls while we were in the garden.'

At this, Douglas whooped in delight. 'What? Bella and Lettie? Which one came out top?'

'He did not say. Knowing father he was viewing them as a farmer would a cow.'

'Lettie would win that beauty competition hands down. She is a fine heifer. Bella is more for show — lean, finely trimmed and docile.'

Not laughing along with his friend, James rubbed his forehead pensively. 'What can I do, Douglas?'

Finally, Douglas took on a more serious tone and said, 'Perhaps you should ask Bella. You know she is keen on you, and there is no better girl around.'

James sighed. 'That may be so but I doubt she will want to marry yet either.'

'Well, get engaged and join the army volunteers with me. We shall sign up for two years.'

'That is a long engagement. I cannot see why any woman would wait that long.'

'Oh, you could come back and marry her in between...then be off again. We shall have a blast.'

'A blast? I like the sound of that,' James said, thinking only of the volunteers. He had no intention of getting engaged to either Arabella or Letitia.

Chapter Five

The next afternoon brought an extra job for Emily, a fortnightly chore that she looked forward to doing – delivering eggs to Mrs Barker in the next village. The journey from Flemsbury to Sidmouth comprised a succession of roaming lanes bordered by lustrous hedgerows thick with flora and wildlife. As Emily strolled along, she breathed the scent of honeysuckle and hedge mustard while serenaded by yellowhammer birds. After walking a good mile from the farmhouse, she reached a fence signalling the start of the final stretch. Carefully she climbed onto the top step and lowered the basket onto the ground the other side before sitting on the horizontal rail for a rest.

From her perch, she studied the landscape ahead taking in the many thousands of acres of barren fields, land that had once been fertile but now served as hunting ground. On the horizon, grey clouds marred the sky as a steam locomotive trundled through the countryside on its way to Birmingham. It was too far away to hear so didn't spoil the natural soundscape, but Emily knew that the time would come when the engines' whistles would drown out those of the birds.

Emily didn't share her brother's excitement over the constant modernisation of life and refused to see it as progress. How could progress fill the air with dirty smoke or scar fields with iron rails? Every invention seemed to move people further from nature be it trains, farming equipment and even craftwork. One day, she supposed, cows and hens would be housed in factories and their milk and eggs collected by machinery. And it would be the same for people, no longer working in the fresh air but locked in damp and dirty buildings from morning till night. The possibility of her being one such worker sent a shiver down Emily's spine, and she shook the image away before climbing down from the fence to continue her journey.

Another ten minutes of her stroll took Emily to the final strip of road leading to her destination. Ahead could be seen a cluster of stone buildings interspersed with dark specks. As Emily came nearer, the specks began to move around and then morph into discernible shapes the largest of which were horses. One of the smallest shapes began to run towards Emily and she lifted the basket of eggs onto her shoulder in preparation.

'Morning, Ted,' she laughed. She rubbed the head of the small white terrier leaping at her with such excitement. 'What a greeting this is?'

'Morning Emily,' a man's voice called from inside the largest building.

'Morning Mr Barker. How's the Arab?' she asked, looking at the large brown animal obscuring her view of the blacksmith.

'Ah, these pampered ponies and their tantrums will be the death of me. Good for nothing but show. Give me a work horse any day.'

Emily smiled at the horse's high-flowing tail before walking through the open door of the second-largest building. Laying the basket of eggs on the wooden table stretching nearly the entire width of the room, she greeted the woman already in the kitchen. Mrs Barker smiled warmly as she placed a large plate next to the basket. Next, she cut a piece from the pie resting on the plate and handed it to Emily.

'Sit yourself down, girl. I'll pour you some tea to go with it.'

Her mouth already watering, Emily did as she was told. After taking a bite from the slice of pie, she paused to enjoy the sensation of the warm stewed apple in her mouth. Puddings were a luxury in her house as her mother believed they got more than enough sugar from dairy products. Emily supposed that was why she was so thin compared to Lilly who was able to tuck into rich pastries every day.

Mrs Barker took the eggs from the basket and then sat opposite Emily so they could share each other's news. Of course, it was the older woman who did most of the talking while the younger one listened and nodded politely. As the only woman in the household, Cassie Barker took hold of any opportunity to "have a natter".

'Our Tommy will be on dry land by now and on his way home,' she said proudly. 'I've spent all week cleaning his room ready for when he gets here as he'll want a long sleep after the journey he's had.'

Emily nodded, smiled and looked interested while trying not to think about the apple pie left on the large plate. Suddenly, a stream of curses could be heard outside and Cassie's attention was forced back to her husband.

'That man needs to rub his mouth with salt using words like them when we have visitors.'

'Don't worry, Mrs Barker,' Emily said, laughing. 'I hear enough of that in the market.'

'Aye, but not at home, do you? Not with you being brought up so righteous.'

'I'm sure Mr Barker didn't mean for me to hear. That's a grand-looking horse he's having to shod.'

'One from the manor. You know how much he hates those types. Swears they look down their long noses at him.'

Emily laughed again. 'Is it one of his hunting horses?'

'Not this one. It belongs to the son. He came here demanding he goes in front of the other horses. When Bill said no, he just threw a shilling into the air as if that settled it. Them people think money buys anything.'

'Is he like that too?' Emily asked, disappointed to hear the negative portrayal of James. 'I've heard bad things about the father.'

'Well, Charles Murdoch is a miserable so-and-so, but he has suffered great losses over the years. I don't think he has much love for the son he has left.'

'Why do you say that? Surely, his son would mean everything to him.'

'It is said that Master James' resemblance to his mother irked Charles after she left him so he sent him away to boarding school so as not to look at him daily.'

'That's terrible but why did the mother leave? I thought she died?'

Cassie looked at Emily curiously. 'Who told you that?'

'Er, I heard it in the market.'

'Not that I've heard. She left ten years ago and no one has seen her since.'

Emily felt the blood rushing to her cheeks. Was it embarrassment or anger? She wondered if anything James had told her was the truth and was about to bring up the subject of his siblings when she heard movement outside.

'That'll be him coming back for his horse now,' Mrs Barker said, rolling her eyes.

'Who?'

'James Murdoch, of course. That'll be a carriage dropping him back.'

'But you said ... I thought Mr Barker ...'

'Of course, he took the money, dear. Did you think he hadn't?'

Panic pounding inside her head, Emily jumped out of the chair. 'Pardon me! I must go, Mrs Barker. Thanks for the pie.'

'Hold on. I ain't given you your basket back yet.'

'Don't worry. I'll collect it again,' she said.

'But it won't take ...' Mrs Barker trailed off as she watched Emily disappear through the open door.

***

As soon as she entered the kitchen, Lilly slumped into a chair and kicked off her shoes much to the annoyance of Mrs Mallard who had tired of complaining about the odour reaching her cooking. Adam, the only other person in the kitchen, was too absorbed in his paper to care either way.

'What's the latest, Adam?' Lilly said, rubbing her stockinged feet.

'Nothing for you to worry your pretty head about, sexy,' he replied without lifting his head. 'Just some whore house got burnt down in the city.'

'I'll not have that language heard in my kitchen,' Mrs Mallard snapped. 'And you treat Lilly with some respect, d'ya hear?'

After giving her a toothless grin, Adam blew a kiss to Lilly who retaliated by throwing a tea towel at him. This time the cook merely rolled her eyes. She had been an authority figure to the two young servants since they started at the house before they were even out of childhood. As they had grown up, she had grown weary of keeping any silly behaviour in check. At the grand age of sixty-five, she had seen servants come and she had seen them go, and lately, more had gone than had stayed. Lilly and Adam would not be around for much longer.

'That's not the kind of news I was asking about, and you know it,' Lilly said quietly, wary of the cook's ears. 'Are there any jobs going yet?'

Adam put down his paper and shifted to the seat next to Lilly. 'Give us a kiss and I'll tell you.'

'Not on your life. I shall find out myself if you won't tell me.'

'Alright, darling. Just for you.' He moved his head towards her. 'Well, while I was waiting for her ladyship to finish shopping, I could hear a lot of banging coming from down the road so I asked another driver and he said they were building a foundry and it'd be ready first thing September. They're sure to want a lot of workers as it's gonna be big.'

'A foundry. They'll be offering good money for those jobs. Sam and I could afford somewhere decent to live if I could work too.'

The young man laughed. 'You are full of hope, aint you? There's gonna be thousands of men going for those jobs so he better get his name down quickly.'

Lilly didn't respond because she was no longer listening to the man who had given her the news. She was busy making plans in her head.

***

By the time Emily reached the end of the first lane, she could feel liquid droplets trickling down her arms. She had run virtually the entire mile from the Barkers' house and at one point the consumed apple pie almost came back into her mouth possibly due to nerves as much as overexertion. Not yet having the energy to climb over the gate separating her from the next path, she sat on the grass to recover some breath and create an excuse for leaving without the basket. Perhaps she'd overreacted. If she'd remained in the kitchen, the likelihood was that no one but Mrs Barker would have seen her yet by running outside, she had increased the chances of him passing her by accident. She needed to hurry home.

A few seconds later, she gathered herself together and mounted the first rung of the gate when suddenly she heard horse's hooves coming from some way back from where she had run. The sound was getting louder and louder therefore the distance between them was closing. Normally a passing horse rider would not bother her as most were known to the area and none of those were considered a threat. All the same, she hurried over the gate and began running again before realising she had not recovered enough of her breath to continue. As she slowed down, so did the sound of the horse behind her. She stopped but the horse carried on for a few more seconds. A moment of silence followed before a familiar voice shouted her name.

'Why are you running from me?' James called out to her before dismounting and walking as far as the stile.

Emily reversed her steps to make herself heard. 'I was hurrying home, not from you. It is difficult to believe but I do have an existence beyond you.'

'May I accompany you,' he asked, ignoring the sarcasm. 'This is a lonely path, and I hate to think of you walking alone.'

Emily wanted to mock him and boast that she had walked that same path alone dozens of times. Yet something stopped her. Instead, she pointed out that the gate was an obstruction. 'The horse will not be able to jump that.'

Without replying, James walked over to the fence and pulled back a bolt buried under a tangle of twigs. After opening the gate, he led the horse through to the other side to join Emily who was already walking on, furious with herself for forgetting about the bolt.

'You look tired. Please sit on Majesty for the remainder of your journey. She is a good girl and will not bolt.'

Emily gazed up at the Arabian mare she had seen in Mr Barker's forge. It was the most beautiful horse she had ever set eyes on, muscular yet elegant, with its glossy chestnut coat perfected by a luscious mane. She shook her head. 'I'm not good with horses I don't know. Besides, there isn't much further to walk now.'

'Where have you been hurrying home from?' he asked, without further mentioning the horse.

Now Emily wished she hadn't waited for him. With no time to think of a lie, she tried being vague. 'I delivered eggs to a family in the next village.'

'Well, we must have been in the same place. I have just come from Sidmouth. Where were you? Actually, that is the only place for miles back there.'

Knowing there was little point in denying it, Emily nodded. 'Yes, I was there too.'

He clapped his hands together. 'How extraordinary! Which family did you deliver to?'

Burning up inside, Emily reacted with irritation. 'Why do you ask me that? There must be dozens of families there.'

James laughed. 'It is little more than a hamlet, Emily. There cannot be more than five houses. Hold on. You were running from me, were you not?'

'No, I wasn't.' But Emily's neck and cheeks, which were the colour of rhubarb stalks, gave her away. She braced herself for more teasing.

But James was no longer laughing. Rather his expression suggested that he was offended more than amused. He shook his head but said nothing. From that moment they walked on with nothing but the horse's clopped steps breaking the silence. Eventually, they reached the last part of the journey and as the lane was straight and the way ahead clear, James offered to watch Emily walk it alone.

'If anything happens, I shall be with you in an instant,' he said, his voice serious but kind.

Tired of the uncomfortable silence, Emily was more than happy to accept his offer yet confused by his change in tone. 'Thank you but what is the matter? You seem sad.'

James smiled faintly. 'Because I have feelings for you which you do not share. Please accept my apologies for harassing you.'

'But you haven't been harassing me. We spent time talking, that's all.'

'Then why do you avoid me?'

The direct question left Emily tongue-tied and filled with an irrational sense of guilt. Being truthful would be the simplest answer. 'When I saw you with that lady at church, I decided it would not be proper to be alone with a man who belongs to someone else.'

'But that is preposterous. I was also at church with my friend, Douglas, but I do not belong to him. Emily, listen,' he said, stretching his arms to bring her closer to him. 'My heart belongs to you only.'

Emily could hear the beating of her heart as she felt his gentle but firm hands on her shoulders. As she met his gaze, a bolt of electricity engulfed her body but before she could look away again, he pressed his lips to hers. The few seconds it took before she pulled back were long enough to show her feelings but he apologised regardless.

'Forgive me, Emily. I had no right.'

She touched his hand and then walked on alone.

***

John Mayer blew the last of the candles out and made his weary way up the stone steps into the bedroom he shared with his wife. Mara was already huddled under the heavy woollen blankets but was still waiting for him to join her before giving in to the night. As usual, once he had laid his aching body on the mattress he unloaded the various worries that had troubled him throughout the day.

'She's been talking to that lad from the manor again. I saw them walking down the lane together and they were far closer than they ought to be. That's the third time now so it can't be a chance meeting.'

When there was no reply, he looked over at his wife. 'You knew about this, didn't you?'

Mara turned her face towards him and smiled. 'I didn't know who it was, but the way she's been acting lately, up and down, struggling to eat her food, taking that much longer getting changed to go to the meadow. Yes, it was clear she was taken with someone.'

'Not just anyone though. Charles Murdoch's son. He'll be up to no good for certain and she's too innocent to know.'

'Don't worry, John. She's a good girl and wouldn't do anything daft.'

'I wish I was as sure about that as you are.'

'Listen, John, It'll pass as quickly as it started. He'll be married off in a couple of years and she'll forget all about him.'

'He will, alright but I'm not so sure about our daughter. That girl's been floating around like a fairy. She's got stars in her eyes and is heading for a fall. We should put a stop to it before anything bad happens.'

'Em's not a child anymore. She works hard every day and we can't begrudge her a bit of happiness when she has a few hours leisure.'

'It's just that I don't want her getting ideas above her station. I know what those money men are like. They play around with the pretty village girls, sowing oats and breaking lives. I've a good mind to go and see Mr Murdoch about it.'

Mara gasped. 'You can't do that. If you make him angry he could change his mind about the extra time he's given us.'

'Six months! What good is that?'

'It is six months better than what we had, otherwise, he'd evict us before Christmas.'

'He wouldn't dare because we've got rights. That's what Jim said.'

'That is as maybe, John. But we haven't got the money to use them. Charles Murdoch is not the man his father was. He doesn't care about his tenants and feels no sense of duty to the village. Maybe this is a blessing in disguise. Things will only get worse if we stay.'

'Well, that's not going to help in the meantime, not so far as the son is concerned. Oh, daughter of mine! Why can't you go with a local lad? There's plenty around.'

Suddenly, Mara sat upright and smiled. 'The Barker's son is back from working at sea and is sure to be looking for a girl after so long without.'

'What makes you so confident our daughter will like him any more than the other village lads?'

'Because he's nothing like the others. He's sailed around the world so everyone will be fascinated by him. And, he'll be a good-looking man if he takes after his father. Local girls will be fighting over a handsome adventurous sailor like him. And Emily is the prettiest girl in the village.'

'That she is,' said John as he yawned. 'But they haven't even met or at least not since she was a babe.'

'Don't worry about that,' Mara said, kissing him on the cheek. 'Leave that to me.'

John squeezed his wife's hand. 'You're a diamond, Mara. Now I can sleep.'

Chapter Six

Daylight was already fading when Emily approached the beginning of the meadow. The cows had been temperamental during their afternoon milking causing her to fall off the stool more than once. It was so late when she finished her work that she considered running to meet James in her milk-stained dairy clothes. However, she was well aware of the way her brother gazed in wonder at Lilly with her flattering clothes and perfectly styled hair. So, at the risk of missing James, Emily spent far more time than usual preening herself before leaving the bedroom. She couldn't meet her mother's eyes as she rushed out of the house.

The sky was patterned with red and golden streaks as the sun began its journey to the distant world. Summer solstice had gone by and the nights were already drawing in. The trees were in full bloom but soon they would drop their fruit. It was usually Emily's favourite time of the year and she wished she could capture every natural scene in her memory like a painting. But this harvest brought with it something more, a sensation she had not felt before. Each fallen apple had its own identity with a unique shape and shade. It was as though she were viewing the world through an invisible lens which enhanced the scene that once looked so familiar to her. And there was something else that was new – James. They had met regularly since he kissed her for the first time that day and she could still feel the tingles that went through her body like magic dust sprinkled over her. During the next few weeks, the kisses were longer and deeper leaving Emily with a growing need for more. Yet she never let him go too far. Her dignity was still intact.

Suddenly her nose was itching and she brushed away the purple thistle tickling it. 'Don't!' she cried, even though she could not help but giggle. 'You'll give me hay fever.'

James, who had seemed to appear from nowhere, was grinning at her. 'I can't help it,' he said. 'You have such a pretty little nose I want to break it off and take it away with me.'

She rolled her eyes in mock irritation. 'And how would I breathe without my nose, smarty pants?'

'Through your pretty mouth, my sweetness. Those lips will need something to do while I'm away.'

The last few words were upsetting enough for Emily, but the fact that they were spoken without a change in tone was even worse. Was she about to come crashing back down to earth? Although her heart was already sinking, she tried to act as nonchalant as him when she asked, 'What do you mean "away"?

'I'm going to be a soldier for a while. There's little for me to do around here.'

'But what about your father's estate? I thought you were the sole heir now. Won't you have to take over?'

'Yes, but not for a few years as my father is not very old. If I stay here with nothing to do, I shall spend too much time partying and that won't be good for my health.'

And there it was, she thought - the end of a ridiculous dream. She lay back on the grass and looked up at the clouds like she used to do before he came. But the white swirls were too blurry to distinguish anything so she closed her eyes and felt the tears trickling down her cheeks. 'I knew this could not last,' she said.

James lay down next to her and wiped the tears away softly. 'Do not cry, my love. I am not going away for long and not even very far. Just Scotland and I'll be back for Christmas.' It will be the same as being a student only I will hold a sword rather than a pen.'

'But why? There is no war.'

'Oh, I shall only be a volunteer, not a real soldier. That is why it is not far and Scotland is somewhere I have never been. It has so many beautiful parts that I plan to see. We shall be based in the Highlands so climbing Ben Nevis will be my first priority and then as many lochs as I can in the time I am there.'

Emily didn't see the point in joining the army only to live in Scotland but decided that his was a world she wasn't meant to understand. Before meeting him, she had never had a conversation with somebody from the gentry class or even been in their presence apart from at church. In the same way, she wondered what he made of her or why he was even spending time with her. Maybe he regarded her as a source of amusement while living at home with his father. Filled with indignation, she considered going back to the farmhouse early so she could be the one to leave first. After all, it was she who had arrived first. Yet, that had been her special place for a few years long before she knew of his existence. Such conflicting thoughts churned inside her head as she pretended to listen to James planning his upcoming tour of Scotland.

'I see I am boring you again,' he said, interrupting her private thoughts.

'A bit,' she replied, finding honesty easier than continuing with the pretence. 'How can I share your excitement when I am not part of your adventure? Your plans do not include me.'

He leaned towards her and kissed her head. 'Oh Emily, you are so wrong. I shall take you with me here,' he said, holding his hand to his chest. 'Listen! Wherever I go, and with every beat of my heart, I shall feel you beside me.'

'And what about my heart?' she said. The thought of not seeing him again sparked a need in her that she had not thought was there. Slowly she undid the top buttons of her dress and, taking his hand, placed it on her naked breast. She closed her eyes and parted her lips in anticipation.

James kissed her gently before withdrawing his hand and pulling her upright. 'Let us not give way to temptation yet. You must remain my beautiful maid for a while longer.'

Despite James' respectful behaviour, Emily was overcome with embarrassment and shame. She had offered herself to him and he had rejected her. There was no way back. He now held the upper hand because she had given it away. It was time to go home.

James accompanied Emily back across the meadow though most of the journey was walked in silence. Finally, as they neared the stile he took hold of her cold hands and rubbed them between his own. 'Next time we meet, I want to see you in warmer clothes. These late summer evenings can turn chilly.'

'It will be winter soon enough,' she replied quietly.

'Do I hear melancholy in your sweet voice? Dearest Emily, I am not going away for another week and shall be back before Christmas,' he said, his eyes burning with a seriousness she had not seen before. Then he kissed her gently before placing his hands around her slim waist and lifting her over to the other side.

Emily attempted a smile, but it pushed too hard against her despondency. All she could manage was to say, 'Goodbye, James.'

***

When Emily finally returned to the house, she was surprised to see a young man sitting at the table. He stood up immediately and offered the vacant chair to Emily who quickly shook her head and looked at her mother sitting across the table from him.

'Emily, luv. You remember Tommy Barker, don't you? He's just come here to bring the yarn because his mother is not feeling well. Tommy's just back from Jamaica. He's got a lot of interesting tales to tell about that place. You wouldn't believe it.'

The man who remained standing gave Emily an awkward smile, revealing small white teeth. His fair hair was cut short drawing attention to soulful grey eyes. He hardly looked familiar, but remembering her manners, Emily managed to speak.

'Hello, Tommy. It's good to see you again. How long are you home?'

'About three months. I've signed up for a voyage to Australia in October so that'll be a long un. We'll likely be away for a few years.'

'Now, that's enough talk of leaving when you've only just arrived,' Mrs Mayer said, as she got to her feet. 'I'm going outside to do some washing so why don't you make a pot of tea, luv and cut a slice of bread and cheese for Tommy, too.'

'But mother, I must ...' Emily's voice trailed off as her mother disappeared through the back door. Still filled with misery after her latest experience with James, all she wanted to do was bury her head under a blanket and cry until every tear had left her eyes. Instead, she turned to

Tommy and, shrugging her shoulders, told him to sit back down. Fighting the urge to follow her mother into the garden, Emily dragged her feet over to the table picked up the teapot and, after refilling it with boiling water from the stove, sat down too. She took as much time as she could pouring out the tea and offering him the milk jug and then sugar bowl hoping to hear her mother returning to the kitchen. But once the clinking of china had ceased, the only sound was feet tapping lightly under the table. Instinctively, Emily glanced down at the floor causing him to cough and cross his legs.

'Sorry,' he said. 'I drive my shipmates mad with my dancing feet.'

Feeling guilty for making him feel the need to apologise, Emily smiled. 'I can't believe you spend much of your time dancing.'

'Only with the trots,' he said, before apologising again when noticing her confused face. 'I'm forgetting myself. You get used to being around men and losing your manners.'

'Aren't there any women on the ship?' Emily said, her eyes widening.

'Once in a blue moon we'll get some church types or wives joining their husbands in India and Africa, but it's not safe enough for them really. To be frank, it's dangerous enough for us.'

'Really!' Despite Emily resenting her mother's blatant attempts at matchmaking, she couldn't help but be intrigued by the man who so matter-of-factly talked about such faraway places, places that were only shapes and words on an atlas to her. Emily had never been beyond the county's parameters, let alone as far as the ocean. How many times in her short life had she laid down on the grass and watched in wonder as the swallows gathered together ready to fly to warmer climates? She could only dream of such places. 'What's it like in Africa? Have you seen a lion?'

'No, but there are plenty of mussies that can be just as deadly,' he said with a grin.'

'Mussies?'

'Mosquitoes. Their bites can give you Yellow Fever. A man's got a far greater chance of dying that way than by a lion.'

'Have you ever been bitten by one?'

'By a lion?'

Emily laughed out loud. 'A mosquito, silly. You wouldn't be here if it had been a lion.'

'How do you know one of these tappers isn't wooden?' he said, pointing to his feet.

'Because they sound too soft and I'm not stupid.' But she could not prevent her eyes from falling on the small scar above his left eye.

He noticed. 'I got smashed by a loose mast,' he said, touching the scar.

'Oh no. That sounds terrible. Were you very injured?'

'Not really. You get used to masts flying around. As long as they don't knock you overboard.'

She smiled. 'Oh, I nearly forgot.' She cut him a piece of the cheese which had been lying untouched.

He took the tea plate from her and bit half of the slice in one go. 'Mmm! This is what I miss more than anything when I'm away — fresh food. The galley rats are better fed than us.'

Despite loving all God's creatures, the mention of rats made Emily shiver. She'd heard too many tales about ship rats carrying diseases to unsuspecting countries across the world. 'Do the rats ever bite you?'

'Na! They're far too scared to come within two yards of us. It's only the droppings we see, not them.'

There was no need for Emily to ask what he meant by 'droppings' and she decided to change the subject. 'Do you think you will ever come back here to live for good?'

On hearing her question, Tommy's eyes took on a pensive glaze although his lips remained upturned. After a long pause, he answered. 'I can't imagine it, to be truthful to you. If I could choose anywhere to settle, it would probably be St Kitts because it's as close to a paradise as you could ever find on this earth.'

Emily fought back the urge to argue accepting that not everyone shared her high opinion of Flemsbury. 'Is it really? I have not heard of it.'

'Well, it's one of the colony islands in America.'

'America. Are there slaves there?'

'No, of course not. There ain't been any slaves in our colonies for years only the Spanish islands and in America.'

Emily had learnt much about the abomination of the slave trade from her mother whose own grandparents had been very active in the calls for abolition. 'What happened to the slaves in the colonies? Did they go back to Africa?'

'I don't think so. Most wouldn't have a clue as to what Africa is as they were born in St Kitts. Now, they work and are paid as any other man.'

'I'm glad. Africa sounds very dangerous with all the lions and mosquitos. Are there lions in St Kitts too?'

He grinned. 'No, only monkeys, lizards and birds of every colour in the rainbow. You should see the size of the flamingos. They are as tall as I am.'

Emily thought that unlikely and hadn't seen a flamingo anyhow yet she could not help but be impressed by Tommy's enthusiasm, and there was some authenticity to what he said. In contrast, James talked about other countries as though they were merely destinations, feathers to put in his cap. Tommy spoke from experience and genuine love and respect for the places he had been.

'I can see you are not impressed,' he said.

For a second, she was confused having mentally moved on from the flamingo comment. 'That's not true. They sound incredible, but to me, nothing is more wonderful than hearing a blackbird singing in the evening.'

'Oh yes. And I bet he sings a special melody for you, Emily.'

Hearing the unexpected remark, similar to those she'd heard so many times from James, Emily might have thought all men's brains were born with the same list of flattering words and phrases. Yet there was a playful innocence to Tommy's tone which did not cause her heart to flutter or blood to rise into her cheeks. 'You tease but I believe beauty is everywhere if you look hard enough. You do not need to search the world over.'

For a short while, he did not answer but merely fiddled with a piece of bread left on his plate. His expression suggested that he was considering what Emily had said. Then he nodded. 'I admire you, Emily. You have been blessed with the ability to recognise what so many others cannot.

I am but a simple man with whatever senses I possess now dampened through harsh storms and burning rays.' At last, he put the bread in his mouth and then stood up. 'I guess I should be going. Thank your mother for the bread and cheese ... and you too for the hospitality.'

'Goodbye, Tommy. It was nice to meet you.' Emily was surprised at his sudden decision to leave though relieved that she would soon be alone. 'Look after yourself, now.'

'Goodbye.' He picked up the scarf lying on the back of the chair, tied it around his neck, and then moved towards the door before stopping with his back to Emily. 'I'm sure we'll see each other again before October. At least, there's a couple of women who are sure to see to it that we do.' He turned and grinned.

She smiled and nodded.

He winked. 'Bye, Emmy.'

Chapter Seven

It was market day in Flemsbury and the square was bustling with life and the air a mix of flower scent, animal smells and freshly baked bread. Sellers and buyers battled to make themselves heard over the cries of rivals besides hens, cockerels and cattle. Having left Sam at the farm, the rest of the family brought their goods to trade with the customers who'd come from miles around. With Emily and his wife walking alongside him, John Mayer steered his cart to a space on the edge of the melee where they set up their stand between one selling linen and another pots and pans. John took up his position beside the vegetables while Mara unwrapped the dairy products. It was Emily's job to model and sell the dozens of straw hats she'd so skilfully created. The late summer sun was blazing down without obstruction and spirits were high amongst the traders as was common at the start of the day. As in church, people of all classes assembled close together but were no longer separated by pews and aisles.

Emily's curls fell like golden tassels from the straw hat keeping the warm rays from her face. It had not been Emily's choice to wear the accessory, preferring her hair to flow freely when not hidden under her dairy cap. However, Emily's parents insisted on her covering at least part of her hair while out with them in public although their reasons were not only related to morals or reputation. Rather, it was a bonus that the sight of Emily drew the attention of admiring men and envious women to the bundle of similar hats she was marketing, and by midday, only a few remained. Emily herself had been sceptical about trying to sell summer hats when they were unlikely to be worn until the following summer but many were bought as early Christmas presents.

It was an all-round successful day's trading for the Mayer family so Mara, planning a special meal to celebrate, was bartering with a meat seller while John treated himself to a tankard of ale. Emily was left alone to dream away the remainder of the working day and she aimlessly surveyed what remained of the people still milling around the market. Peering through a gap in the square, she caught sight of a young woman dressed in elaborate clothes - an emerald green dress buffeted out at the back and a black velvet hat perched on rolls of glossy auburn hair. She was holding a bunch of roses which she was closely examining. At first, Emily thought the woman was alone which would have been extremely unusual but, as the gap widened, she could see a nearby gentleman wearing equally grand attire. Eventually, the man paid for the flowers and the couple began moving through the crowds towards Emily. Combing fingers through her hair and wiping the sweat from her face with a cloth, Emily prepared herself for a possible though unlikely late sale.

'Oh do look at these hats. Are they not sweet?' the woman said. 'Should I try it on?'

'I hardly think it will fit unless you let down your hair,' the man said with a laugh.

When the woman looked at Emily her expression changed slightly before she resumed her mocking tone. 'Well, it might do for the fancy dress ball if I go as an urchin girl.'

'You shall never pass for one, Arabella. It would be better to buy a crown.'

'I think you should try it on, Douglas,' she said, raising her arm to reach him. As they wrestled playfully, the hat ripped at the brim. 'Oh dear. Well, they cannot be very well made.' She dropped the hat on the ground and began to walk away.

For a few seconds, Emily watched while the man appeared unsure of the right thing to do. Then, the other woman called him and he rushed to her side. At that point, the rage that had been contained within Emily's hot and tired body erupted.

'Wait!' she shouted running after them. 'You damaged this hat so you must pay for it.'

The couple stared at her in astonishment as did most of the people in the square. 'I beg your pardon,' the woman said.

'You must pay for the hat that you damaged. It is no good to me now.'

'It was no good before I touched it. Perhaps you should find an easier way to make a few pennies.'

'It was fine before you played tug of war with it. Let's see how your hat looks after it's been pulled around.' She reached up for the black velvet hat but was stopped when somebody grabbed both her arms.

A middle-aged woman pulled Emily back from the couple. 'Let them go, luv. They're not worth the trouble.'

'Hello. What is going on here?' a man could be heard saying behind some bystanders.

Emily didn't have to turn around to know who the voice belonged to. By the time she had, James was standing with the well-dressed couple. When he saw Emily his face dropped and he quickly looked away taking a step back so he was once again hidden from view.

At last, the other man pulled out a shilling and handed it to Emily. 'For the hat.' Then the three friends walked away together.

***

Sam tied up the last rick and lifted it onto the others while Lilly looked on in admiration. During the eighteen months they'd been together, she'd felt the difference in his body as he held her and in his face when they kissed. The first time he spoke to her he was still a teenager with gangly arms and legs yet a chubby face. Having been an early developer herself, as well as a year older, they were an odd pair in their early dating days. Eventually, Sam morphed into the lean, chiselled young man as tall as he was strong. But he was still more son than lover and she knew it would take a lot to persuade him to leave the nest.

It had been so different for her. Living and working at Bamley Hall changed her life in so many ways. The opportunity to leave home at the tender age of nine was something she'd grabbed with both hands and feet. As one of five children, her family were not just poor, they were wretched and made worse by her father's reckless behaviour. He was prone to drink away any money that came his way before taking his guilt out on the children, in particular, the eldest, Lilly. As she grew older, Lilly's resentment fell equally on her mother whose weakness disgusted her. What was the point of having children if you were unwilling to protect them? Lilly vowed never to be that person.

Her parents did not even allow her to attend Sunday school leaving her humiliated by her illiteracy when she began work. The charitable nature of Lady Fortesque allowed her to join the daughters in their classes and Lilly soon realized that she was far from the stupid girl she'd assumed herself to be. Even better, she'd learned many practical skills which should always help her find employment elsewhere. It might not be so easy for Sam. There were no farms where she wanted to go.

'It won't be much longer,' Sam said, as though reading her thoughts. 'The lease on the farm is only being renewed for a year so we'll likely all have to leave then.'

Lilly's heart sank. 'But I don't want to wait another year, Sam. I want to go soon, next month ... now.'

'You know I can't go now,' he said.

She rolled her eyes. 'And you know I don't expect us to go now. I'm trying to make you understand how much I yearn to move on with my life, to start the next part away from being a servant girl.' She stepped forward. 'With you.'

Sam wrapped his arms around her and kissed the top of her head softly. 'Don't you think I want that too? But the time has to be right. It's not just my parents but Emily too. I have to make sure they are secure somewhere before abandoning them. And you are not so bad off in your job for now. The longer you stay, the more you can put by for us to use for somewhere to live. It won't be wasted time.'

Lilly knew what Sam said was sensible. She'd been to London enough times to know that many people lived in little more than slums as seedy as they were uninhabitable. A large proportion of those were people just like them who had already migrated there from rural areas. The houses some had ended up in were squalid, cramped and even disease-ridden. Unless she and Sam were fully prepared, they could end up giving up as soon as they got there.

Sensing that he was once again winning the argument, Sam moved the conversation on slightly. 'What's the latest gossip on those spoilt sisters you have to clean up after?'

'Well, Arabella is keen on the squire's son and hoping they will get engaged soon. I've never seen him though he's supposed to be rather handsome.'

The mention of the squire brought a frown to Sam's youthful face. 'If he's anything like his pa, she'd be better to keep away from him.'

'I don't know about that, but he certainly sounds immature and spends much of the time drunk as far as I can make out.'

'How do you know if you haven't seen him'

'Adam knows everything there is to know about the comings and goings of each family member. When Mrs Mallard isn't listening, he tells me all the gossip. Besides, he often sees James Murdoch walking around doing nothing since he came back from university, aside from getting drunk that is.'

'That's the trouble with his type. They ain't got no need to work to get money for food and somewhere to live cos it's already there for them. I'd rather have a point to my life even if it is to work till my bones are brittle.'

'But your bones won't get brittle if I have anything to do with it,' Lilly replied, pinching his arm. 'That is what machines are for.'

Sam grinned. He could not argue with Lilly's point believing as he did in the benefits of industrial change. A farmer's life was hard enough but it was often short or at the very least physically debilitating particularly for smallholders like them. No longer having the help of labourers, he and his father did all the crop work themselves. His father was still reasonably able-bodied but that did not mean it would be the same for him.

The sound of horses' hooves grew louder, and it was time for the couple to part company. Lilly used her fingers to comb stray bits of hay from Sam's hair before kissing him goodbye and they both ran towards the coach which had just pulled up outside the barn. Sam waved at Adam as he helped Lilly climb into the carriage then stood and watched as it moved off out of sight. From the other direction, the Mayers' horse and cart appeared.

***

The Mayers had been working at the market for so long yet spent little time relaxing once they got home. While John unloaded what remained of the day's goods, Mara began dinner leaving the accounts until daylight. Meanwhile, Emily led the cows into the dairy where she spent the remainder of the daylight but not because of the milking. The whitewashed walls provided a stark barrier between her and the dangerous romance of the world outside which had filled her head with dreams. Within those walls, she could block out the hurt and humiliation and pretend the past few weeks had not happened.

How quickly she had changed from an independent and strong-minded young woman to a girl who was fragile and unrealistic. More than satisfied with the life she had before, she'd not been looking for romance or marriage. He was the one who pursued her and eventually, she'd succumbed to his advances. Had he lost interest? Surely, if he were only interested in the chase, he would have taken her when she'd offered herself. A sudden chill went through her body as she remembered her behaviour the last time on the meadow when she'd placed his hand on her breast.

Was he disgusted by her boldness? What was going through his mind at that point? If she behaved that way with him, perhaps she did with other men. Although she was a cow, that woman at the market would never have degraded herself in that way. And even if she did, it wouldn't matter because she was rich and aristocratic and rich people could do what they wanted. But Emily knew that was unlikely. Aristocratic young ladies had higher standards than dairy maids.

She covered her face with her hands as if she could hide from the unhappy memory. Her self-reproach had not been the plan when she'd sought the sanctuary of the dairy but it was less painful than the other option — that he had never cared for her, that it was merely amusement to a bored young man looking for something to occupy his mind before the next stage of his privileged life. The image of him hiding from her suggested the latter was the case.

***

Adam pulled up outside the market square and an excited Arabella joined Lilly inside. 'What a hoot we had today, Lilly? I cannot wait to tell you everything, but I do not know where to start.'

'It sounds like you had a good deal of fun, miss,' Lilly replied, gearing herself for the usual exhaustive account of Arabella's encounter with her hero. Pummelled with every meticulous detail, she would have to listen intently to be able to comment at the appropriate moments. It was the part of her job she hated more than any other. She settled back while Arabella described their time at the botanical gardens from the transparent activities of playing hide and seek among the plants and statues and getting hopelessly lost in the maze to the subtleties of body language and chosen words.

'He sat closer to me than Letty'. 'He always managed to find me first'. 'He called me "Arabella" several times. Do you think he wanted to say something serious?'

Lilly nodded and answered in the affirmative as if she had any choice in the matter. She'd learnt her lesson years earlier. Once during one of their French classes, Lilly forgetting her place, corrected Arabella's grammar resulting in a tearful tantrum. Following that episode, Lilly was on her best behaviour however it was the end of her French lessons.

By the time they pulled into the long driveway of Bamley Hall, Arabella had moved on to the happenings at the market and was recounting the episode with the straw hat when she suddenly stopped. 'What is the matter, Lilly? Why do you look at me so?'

'I'm sorry, miss but I don't know what you mean. How am I looking at you?'

'As though I were a horrible creature crawling out from a box of old clothes in the attic. Your eyes are wide open and your lips turned down.'

'Oh, forgive me, miss. What you were saying reminded me of a bad experience I had several years ago in the same market square.' Lilly was confident that she would not be asked to go into detail about the fictitious incident.

However, Arabella's eyes narrowed, the excitement gone from them. 'I do not think you are being truthful, Lilly. You think it was terrible of me to do that to the straw hat girl, don't you?'

This time Lilly did not reply. She was not surprised by Arabella's behaviour at the market having witnessed such episodes several times in her time at Bamley Hall. Knowing that 'the straw hat girl' was Emily, rather than reassure her mistress, she also wanted to pull her black velvet hat off and throw it through the carriage window. It was as well that they had arrived at the front entrance and the carriage had stopped. She looked across at Arabella who was staring at the floor.

'I suppose it was rather mean of me,' she said quietly. 'We did not intend for the hat to break and Dougie did pay her for it but ...' she trailed off as Adam opened the door.

Lilly watched Arabella climb down from the carriage and walk into the house by herself. There was no doubt in Lilly's mind that the young woman regretted her actions at the market. Lilly knew her every expression like the back of her own hand. The only mystery was the reason for her regret. Was she genuinely sorry for the distress she'd caused Emily? Or was it all about looking bad in front of her would-be husband James Murdoch?

Chapter Eight

Emily looked at herself in the mirror for the umpteenth time. She had tried on all her dresses and each one made her feel worse than the last. Even her favourite, the powder blue smock, didn't bring out her eyes as usual. Not that she wanted to wear that particular dress as he might be there. Not that she cared if he was there but he might think it was her only dress. Not that she cared what he thought.

There was a knock on the bedroom door and Lilly walked in without waiting to be asked.

'Hurry up, Emily, or we'll miss the acrobats.' She glanced at the pile of clothes on the bed and shook her head. 'I hope you're happy with the one you're wearing because that pile will break the bed if it gets any bigger.'

Emily sighed knowing she would have to make do with the white and yellow cotton outfit. 'Does this make my face look sallow?'

Lilly threw her head back in laughter. 'How could it do that? And you look pretty as a picture so put on your hat and we'll go.'

Another sigh. Emily placed the frilly white cap on top of her pinned-up hair and grimaced at the last sight of herself before leaving the bedroom.

'Doesn't she look pretty, Mrs Mayer?' Lilly said as they entered the kitchen, confident there would be nothing but confirmation in response to her question.

Mara looked up from the table and smiled inside at the rare but thankful sight of Emily's hair pinned back and covered. She had never criticised her daughter despite believing it was better for a young woman not to flaunt her beauty in public, especially if she was unmarried. Would all men view her as good-mannered, hardworking and respectable as Mara knew she was? She worried some might judge her wrongly.

Not that Emily came across many people from outside the family given that she spent most of her free time in the meadow. Mara was grateful for Lilly's insistence that Emily went to the fair with her and Sam. At last, she was making herself visible to potential matches. It was not before time. Mara was confident that many men would be enchanted by Emily's beauty and sweet nature. If any man knew her daughter as well as she did, he could only love her.

***

When they arrived, the fair was already bursting with life and tantalising all the senses with its exhibition of sound and movement. Musical pipes mixed with screams of delighted children filled the warm air rich with the aroma of popcorn and toffee. An artist's palette of colours twirled around the fair as girls and young women in their prettiest dresses moved between stalls and rides. A group of maypole dancers held the attention of a smaller number of spectators. Emily's group headed straight for the largest crowd of people queueing outside a huge white marquee from where screams and loud applause could be heard. At last, after waiting for twenty minutes, those inside shuffled out allowing those queuing to take their places in the recently vacated seats. Lilly rushed in to secure three front-row seats and when everyone was settled, the lights dimmed and the show began again.

Suddenly, waves of flames jumped into the air before falling down and then rising again. The initial gasps and yells from the audience debated when the flames illuminated two jugglers dressed in equally bright red and gold costumes. It was as mesmerising to watch as it was terrifying as the flame-throwers began to seemingly swallow then breathe out fire. They were followed by knife-throwers, contortionists, and plate-spinning until the long-awaited acrobats appeared. The agile and fearless performers stunned the audience with death-defying acts of tossing and catching each other and somersaulting their way to a human pyramid that reached the roof of the marquee. The spectators showed their appreciation by throwing coins and notes into the open sacks taken around by two dwarves on unicycles.

No sooner were they outside in the fresh air that their attention was drawn to a smaller tent where a short line of men and women waited nervously to have their fortunes read. Before Emily had a chance to protest, Lilly grabbed her hand and pulled her over to the queue leaving an amused Sam to wander the fair alone.

'My mother would kill me if she knew I was here,' Emily whispered between giggles.

'Don't you dare tell her then as she will demand Sam stops seeing me. She already thinks I'm a bad influence.'

'Don't worry. I won't tell anyone.' Emily made no response to Lilly's second point as she believed in some ways it was true. 'You are next to go in, Lilly. Are you scared?'

'Of course not. Besides, it's not real. They make everything up.'

'Then why are we wasting our pennies?'

'Because it's fun.'

An opening appeared in the tent and a middle-aged woman in front of them exited with an angry expression on her face. Before the two sides of the tent had time to fall back, Lilly winked at Emily and disappeared inside. Emily waited patiently her curiosity and excitement growing with each passing minute. The middle-aged woman had only been inside for about five minutes but at least fifteen minutes had passed since Lilly had gone in. With nothing to occupy her thoughts, Emily's imagination started to flow. Although merely a foot away from the makeshift door, she could hear nothing coming from within the tent and began to worry that Lilly had been kidnapped. Emily had heard about such crimes committed by travellers but wasn't sure if there was any truth to the rumours. Lilly was a very pretty young woman who always drew admiring looks from passing men. Maybe one of the gypsies had abducted her intending to force her to marry him. Then she noticed Sam and waved to catch his attention. She would tell him how long Lilly had been gone and he could decide what to do. But before he reached her, the tent moved and Lilly came outside laughing.

'Well, that was a waste of time. She kept saying random things hoping one might be right.'

After Lilly's dismal verdict, Emily considered not bothering with the fortune teller but knew Sam would cherish the few minutes alone with Lilly. So she went inside the tent.

A powerful scent of burning incense hit Emily's senses as she gazed at the small figure through the tiny plumes of smoke. An old woman was sitting on a large cushion at the far end of the tent. With a headscarf of silver and gold covering her hair and her body lost inside a long satin cloak only a shrivelled face was showing.

'Sit down, dear,' the old woman said, before holding out the palm of her hand.

Emily sat on a smaller cushion and placed a shilling in the woman's palm. She glanced around the small space expecting to see a crystal ball but there was nothing between her and the older woman. Suddenly, the woman reached out both arms and said, 'Give me your hands.'

Nervously, Emily placed her shaking hands onto the woman's palms which then folded around them. To her surprise, the fortune teller wasted no time before giving her predictions.

'There are two paths ahead of you. Each one leads to a different future. It is for you to choose the one you take.'

Emily glanced up but the woman's eyes were fixed downwards. 'What are those paths?'

'One is flat and one is rocky. The flat path will give you little sadness or joy. The rocky path will give you both.

'Which path should I take?'

'I cannot tell you that. It is for you to find your own way but both will require you to make sacrifices.'

'What kind of sacrifices?'

'Love and honour. You cannot have both.'

The woman dropped Emily's hands and moved her head back. 'Good day to you.'

As Emily emerged from the tent, she was relieved to feel the fresher air on her face, blowing the scent of incense from her nostrils and her stinging eyes. However, she was disappointed by the brief amount of time she was given, less even than the middle-aged woman who was before them in the queue. And Lilly was given fifteen minutes despite not believing a word the fortune-teller had told her. It was a wonder she wasted her hard-earned money on something she viewed with scorn. In contrast, Emily knew she would keep the fortune teller's words in her mind until she saw the next one.

Scanning the crowd in front of her, Emily tried to spot her brother or Lilly but there was no sign of them. Annoyed that they had left her alone so soon, she resigned herself to going home disappointed that her rare trip out had been cut so short. Then she felt a man's hands briefly covering her eyes and, spinning around, saw a grinning Tommy Barker.

'I saw your brother and his sweetheart going into the copse so thought you might need some company.' He bent his arm and, resting hand on hip, winked.

Filled with relief that the day was not over, a beaming Emily threaded her arm through his and forgot all about her brother and Lilly. As they strolled through the fair laughing at the various entertainers, a warmness flowed in Emily's veins. How happy she had been to see Tommy's friendly face rescuing her from the ignominy of being an unaccompanied young woman amongst so many friends and lovers. There were no goosebumps on her flesh or thumps in her chest only a sensation that she was in safe hands.

At the far end of the fair, they came to the main attraction that was gathering large crowds though not all impressed. Four wooden boats were swinging back and forth high in the air and attached to a heavy beam. On either end of each boat sat a young couple in various states of composure. Some laughing, some screaming, some enjoying the sights, some with eyes only for one another. Emily and Tommy glanced at each other, smiled then hurried to the man taking money. They sat at the end facing the whole of the fair and waited with trepidation for their boat to start moving. Then a horn sounded.

As the swaying became steeper, the cries got louder and Emily couldn't help pressing herself against Tommy who didn't seem to mind at all. At the height of each swing there was an almost birds eye view of the whole fair and Emily tried to see her lost companions but quickly felt sick with the effort. Anyway, she thought, they should be able to spot her from miles away so she relaxed and leant her head against Tommy's shoulder.

The ride came to an end all too soon and Emily allowed herself to be lifted from the boat by Tommy who then had to steady her as she was still swaying even on solid ground.

'I'm sorry,' she giggled.

'Don't worry. You are the lightest cargo I have ever carried off a boat,' he said. 'But you would be no good at sea.'

'Emily.' The woman was barely audible through the noise.

They turned to look for the source of the voice and saw Lilly who was standing next to Sam and waving her arms in the air wildly. Quickly they linked arms and threaded their way through the bustle of people to join them unaware of the other person watching them. After standing a mere three feet from Sam for the past few minutes, James Murdoch slipped away into the crowd.

***

As dusk approached, Tommy and Sam headed off to the nearest tavern leaving Emily and Lilly to walk back to the farmhouse where Lilly was spending the night. It was the first time they could compare experiences in the fortune teller's tent. Lilly was the first to recount the relatively long period spent with the old woman.

'As soon as I sat down, she grabbed my hands without even asking which I thought was scary. Then she asked me lots of questions. Did I know someone whose name began with A or M or W? Was I worried about somebody close to me? When I said no to all of them, she babbled something about me having a choice of two paths to follow but couldn't tell me what was on them.'

'*A* might have been Arabella.'

'Or Angus or Albert or a load of poppycock.'

'But you were with her such a long time. Why was that?'

'Well, eventually she told me a little more about those fictitious paths. One led to a dull boring life without risk; the other would be tempting but would lead to disaster. I laughed out loud when she said that. Was I Eve about to be tempted by an apple? She didn't like that at all, so desperately tried to frighten me with talk of dungeons, chains, darkness and even shame which I laughed at again. Finally, she knew I wasn't having any of her nonsense so didn't bother making up any more predictions. How long were you with her? I didn't see you come out.'

'Not almost as long as you. I suppose she could see I was willing to believe anything,' Emily said. 'She told me about two paths as well. One was flat and one rocky.'

'Oh yes. She said that too, and that I would end up taking the flat one. That's when I knew for certain she was guessing.'

'You mean she told you which way you would go? She didn't tell me.'

'As you said, she didn't need to waste any more time convincing you. You were willing to believe anything.'

That seemed a likely explanation to Emily. Lilly may have been a challenge to the fortune teller but one she had not won over. 'Why does taking the flat path mean she was guessing?'

'Because that would mean I'm staying here for the rest of my life. That is not what will happen.'

Emily was surprised at Lilly's interpretation of their nearly similar experiences and wondered if she should be as dismissive as her. But it would be fun imagining what lay on the rocky path. Or who.

As if reading her thoughts, Lilly suddenly grabbed Emily by the shoulders and peered into her eyes.

'I see a man in the near distance on one of the paths. He is tall and slim with short fair hair. Will he be your husband, I wonder?'

'Oh do stop, Lilly,' Emily said, brushing her hands away. 'Tommy and I are friends, that's all. He will be going away again in a few months so there would be little point in marrying him.'

'Unless that's the rocky path. You could go with him.'

'The sea isn't rocky but it is dangerous. I could never imagine myself in the middle of a lake let alone an ocean.'

***

Sam struggled to find sleep that night. For hours he lay in bed listening to the female giggles filtering through the stone wall separating his and Emily's bedrooms. Unlike the Mayers, Lilly was not used to going to bed before midnight living as she did in a house lit with gas where life did not depend on the hours between the first light of dawn and the dark of night. He wondered if Emily was struggling to keep awake or if she was as restless as him. She was probably enjoying the company of a young female with whom she could share her secret thoughts like he had with Tommy earlier. His tales of roaring waves and endless horizons fascinated Sam who had never even seen the sea. While Tommy had travelled thousands of miles in all directions between distant continents, Sam was supposed to feel guilty about moving little more than a hundred miles away. His stories were so detailed that Sam could taste the salt air on his tongue and feel the blistered skin baking under the ubiquitous sun. Their lives were worlds apart, but only one of them had interesting tales to tell. After all, Tommy knew as much about rural life in Flemsbury, having lived there too so there was nothing Sam could tell him that he did not already know.

Not that Tommy was a bragger. Indeed he claimed to miss the vast green fields and home comforts like his mother's pies. But it wasn't enough to stop him wanting to sign up for another voyage which would take him away for two years or more. Although he knew it was selfish, Sam wished that he was back to stay for good as that might make things easier for him. Tommy was strong and used to hard labour which was exactly the sort of man Sam had been looking for to replace him. He wouldn't need lodgings as his family owned a horse which he could use to travel the few miles between the properties. Also, if he stayed around long enough, things might develop between him and Emily and they had seemed happy enough together at the fair. The last thought excited Sam who worried about his sister spending her youth hidden away at the farm. When she did go anywhere like the market, her clothes were tatty and unflattering, in contrast to Lilly who managed to look lovely even at church. It was only because Lilly would not take no for an answer, that Emily agreed to go with them to the fair. She'd spent weeks insisting that she did not want to be a gooseberry yet Lilly managed to persuade her to go at the last minute. He was happy to share his short time with Lilly if it was to find a man for Emily. She was still young, but her prettiness would not last forever. How would she find a husband if the only other place she went was the meadow?

Chapter Nine

The sky was heavy with dark clouds so Emily agreed to wear a shawl on her afternoon walk despite hating the feel of the harsh grey wool against her arms. For Emily, it was a matter of keeping her mother happy and free from worry. Often she would hide the unwanted garment behind a bush and retrieve it on her way home. However, her mother's words were still ringing in her ears.

"A dead dairymaid is of no use to me," she had said, in false jest.

Mara still fussed over her daughter despite knowing it was wrong to keep her cossetted. Equally, Emily accepted that she could be careless often having thrown caution to the wind, when it would have been wiser to have stayed home in the warm and dry. And that day was so dark, she almost gave in to caution but for one thing pushing her on. She hadn't seen the blackbird for a few days and was worried it would fly away forever. If it was there, she would leave some food and go straight back home.

Approaching the stile, she wiped the specks of rain from her long eyelashes to clear her vision. It would be easy to slip off the wet wood and hurt her ankle. She stepped carefully onto the bottom rung and lifted herself over to the other side without mishap. The memory of Tommy's hands around her waist brought a warm glow to her belly. The comfort she'd felt being in his company had given her something to think about. He had taken on the role of her protector even if only for a short time. Did he represent the safe path, the one without joy or pain? Thunder rolling in the distance brought her back to reality, and she reminded herself that Tommy had shown nothing but friendship towards her. He didn't look at her with anything other than brotherly affection and his intentions were always entirely honourable. Perhaps he had a secret wife in one of the many countries he travelled to, she wondered, trying to picture the women of those distant places.

By the time she reached the meadow, the specks of rain had turned into droplets so she stood under an elm tree for some shelter. She didn't want to go home before seeing the blackbird yet there was no sound or sight of her. What if the blackbird was killed by the hawk that had been flying around for the past few weeks? A shiver ran down her back at the horrible thought. Predators and prey were an essential part of life, especially in the countryside, and Emily knew it was unwise to give animals their own identities like she had with the blackbird. Her father was always laughing at her for that reason insisting the blackbirds were likely to be different each time as birds didn't live that long in the wild.

Another clap of thunder, louder this time, made her wrap the shawl even tighter around her shivering body. The wind had picked up and the horizon lit up briefly signalling worse to come. She could not stay any longer as the storm was getting nearer. Soon, it would be dangerous to be so close to the trees. It probably already was.

Leaving the relative shelter of the elm tree, exposed her to the full force of the strengthening gusts and within minutes, she was soaked through and struggling to see the ground in front of her. All around her, simultaneous flashes of lightning and claps of thunder made Emily feel as though she could be trapped in one of the horror stories she'd heard about. Spooked by her own imagination, she turned her head to check that no monster was chasing her through the meadow. As she turned back her foot struck something hard. She knew she was going over and, though everything was in slow motion, was unable to use her hands to break the fall. With a force that knocked the breath from her, she hit the ground.

Confused and frightened, Emily lay face down on the puddled grass while assessing the result of her fall. Apart from a sore knee and dull throbbing in one foot, she was unscathed. At last, she managed to pull herself into a sitting position and prepared to stand and only then did she become aware of the intensity of the pain in her right foot. Any attempt to put weight on it caused her to cry out first in pain then in frustration. Would she have to crawl home? A continuous clap of thunder rolled through the sky towards her, and she pulled the scarf over her face in terror. Through the coarse thread, she could see the dim light fade to darkness then the thunder ceased. Something landed on her shoulder and she shrunk even further within the tiny space she was occupying. A scintilla of warm air brushed her icy hand and then the shawl was moved away from her eyes.

A man was leaning over her, his features blurred behind a watery mask but she knew it was James. Behind him stood the large Arabian horse waiting obediently. Within seconds, she was pulled to her feet and lifted in the air.

'Grab hold of the reins and I shall push you up,' he shouted through the howling wind.

Emily fell sideways on the saddle and grappled through the wet chestnut hair for the reins but couldn't reach them. A huge gust of wind blew her backwards, and she began to slip down the saddle until her foot made contact with the stirrup. Luckily it was the left foot and, grabbing the horse's mane, she pushed down on the stirrup to yank herself up. The reins were pushed into her hands, and the horse began to walk on slowly until it stopped again and her body was being pushed forward. Emily was no longer alone on the horse, and he wrapped his arms around her waist tight enough to keep her secure on the saddle, grab the reins and steer the horse into a gallop.

A stable came into view, and the horse slowed to a canter and then a trot until James slid off the saddle before lifting Emily onto the ground. During the intensity of the last ten minutes or so, she had been aware of nothing except the feel of his body pressed up against hers. Even standing unaided, it was as though the searing pain in her foot was a million miles away or part of a dream. She hardly noticed the drenched shawl being replaced with a dry blanket and the water gently wiped from her face. Her attention was fixed on James removing his own sodden jacket and shirt before drying his chest with the towel he had just used on her face. She knew it was shameful of her not to turn away or cover her eyes with the large blanket that was giving her much-needed warmth, but the image before her was too mesmerising. As if self-conscious, he walked past her and out of sight though not earshot. For a while, she could hear rustling and panting until at last he re-emerged wearing a different shirt.

'That is her tucked up for the night. She deserves a rest after carrying the two of us. We shall use the stallion to get you back home. I keep a change of clothing here,' he said, noticing her confused expression. 'It proves to be useful occasionally. I wish I could offer *you* something to change into.'

Emily smiled awkwardly on hearing the reference to her wet clothes. Nothing was proper about the situation she had found herself in, nor could she envisage a way out without somehow ending up with a tarnished reputation. Should she demand to be taken home? Surely that is what anyone decent would do. She tried to imagine that horrid woman at the market and what she would do if she were in Emily's place. James would surely have taken her back to her palace or wherever it was she lived instead of to that forsaken barn. Yes, he could have taken Emily to the farmhouse rather than place her in such a compromising position. Also, it would be her whose name was sullied. She should be angry at him...but she wasn't.

Feeling his hand on her shoulder, she let him guide her to a corner of the barn farthest from the horses. She sat on one of the bundles of hay, and he sat next to her. For a few minutes, they did nothing but listen to the remnants of the storm that had driven them there. It was James who broke the silence.

'Your foot is swollen and must be extremely painful. It would be better for you to rest it for the next few days.'

'I didn't know you cared for my well-being,' Emily replied, surprised by her own curtness.

James turned to face her. 'Of course, I care for you, Emily. Why would you say such a thing?'

'When I was at the market, you were ashamed to even look at me because you were with your posh friends.' The words were spilling out of Emily's mouth as her brain was pushing her heart to the back. 'It is clear that you only intend talking to me when nobody else can see.'

James' face crumpled. The words had pierced his pretence of ignorance and confusion. He knew full well what Emily meant. 'You are right, Emily. It was disgraceful of me to behave in such a cowardly manner. I did not even realise myself how much I had denied my own feelings for you. When I saw you lying there as I was riding past, for a second I feared something dreadful had happened, even that you were...' He gasped then bit into his knuckles before regaining composure and continuing, 'I was so relieved to find you in good health.'

Again her cheeks were moist but this time not with rain. Her legs were shaking but not from the cold. To hear him speaking so openly about his feelings, sent electricity through her veins. She touched his arm. He lifted his head then moved his face closer to hers until their lips touched. Her hands cupped the back of his head as it moved across her cheeks and down her neck. She inhaled deeply and prepared to give herself to him completely as she felt her cold wet dress being lifted upwards. Her bare skin, no longer chilled by the clammy cotton dress, was warmed by his caress as their bodies came together. As his mouth moved across her cheek and down her neck, she fell back onto the straw and closed her eyes.

They lay in each other's arms their half-naked bodies covered with the blanket. Emily, her head resting on James' bare shoulder, wondered if she would ever feel that happy again. Before she could cherish the moment, his next words thrilled her even more.

'I want you to be my wife, Emily. Will you marry me?'

Emily's rose lips gaped open in surprise then flinging her arms around James, she cried. 'Yes, yes.' Somewhere in the back of her mind, she knew it was crazy but the moment was too perfect to spoil. Wrapped in his arms, she listened as he planned their future together.

'We shall live in London while I complete my Law studies. Then, if you like, we could move back to Flemsbury. I know how much you love living here.'

'London is not a good place to raise children,' Emily said. 'They would miss out on the joys of being a child in the countryside.'

'Yes, you are right,' he said. 'I was one such child having spent a large part of my younger life in boarding schools. However, I shall have to learn a profession, if I am to take care of you.'

'What is wrong with looking after the estate?'

'That will not happen for many years as my father is still young enough to take care of it himself. I cannot rely on him for my future. In fact, I have no desire to follow in his footsteps preferring to make my own way in the world — with you.'

'Your father will not be pleased.'

'My father will be furious. In fact, he will probably disinherit me even though I am his sole surviving heir.' He turned to face Emily. 'Will you still want me if I am a mere pauper?'

Her expression changed to one of indignation. 'What a terrible thing to ask? I would love you even more if that were possible because we would be able to begin our lives together afresh, held back by no honours or class divide. I don't care where we live or what we need to do to stay together.'

'Well, hopefully it will not be as bad as all that. Once I qualify as a lawyer, we shall be able to afford a decent place in Oxford. But until then, we may have to go without small luxuries. He kissed her again. 'What about your family? How will they manage without their pretty milkmaid?'

Emily paused before answering. She had been so overwhelmed with happiness, the effect on her own family had not been considered until that moment. If Charles Murdoch would go as far as cutting off his only heir, he would most likely react as angrily towards her family — with more devastating consequences.

Sensing her concern, James cradled her in his arms. 'You do not have to say anything yet if you are worried about my father. I shall make sure he does nothing to harm anyone in your family.'

'But I need to prepare them if I am to leave.'

'If I go to Scotland as planned, that should be enough time for them. It will also give me the opportunity to write to friends about somewhere to live. I know many people in Oxford. That should take a month or two. Yes, we shall leave straight after I return from Scotland ... in October.'

Emily's beating heart drowned out the guilt festering inside her. 'Will I see you before you go?' Emily said.

He kissed her head. 'If you are able, meet me in the meadow on Friday at the usual time. But I shall understand if you are not there.'

'I'll be there. When will you tell your father?'

James laid back on the straw and fixed his eyes on the rafter above. For a short while, he watched a spider as it crawled along its web to a trapped insect. 'Tomorrow. I shall tell him tomorrow.'

***

It was dark when the carriage pulled up outside the farmhouse. Emily stepped into an empty building as everyone was out searching for her. Suddenly, she remembered that her actions had an effect on other people, and once again guilt and shame rushed through her mind. However, it didn't take long for the carriage light to attract attention, and within a short time, all of the Mayer family members were inside the farmhouse. Nobody had seen the carriage driver which placed Emily in a quandary. It would have been far easier if she had nothing left to hide from her family. But now it was in her power to lie, and a nagging doubt warned her not to tell them the complete truth. Instead, she mixed fact with fiction:

I sheltered under a tree for the entire storm then, as I was running home, fell and hurt my foot. A passing carriage noticed me struggling to walk so brought me home.

Did you know the driver?

No.

Was he a local?

I don't think so as his accent was alien.

Of course, they believed her because she was a trusted daughter and sister, and that only increased her guilt. But for the moment she needed to enjoy the experience in the stables without judgment, reprimand and doubt.

Chapter Ten

The moment Emily stepped into the kitchen, her mother knew she'd changed. It was in the way her feet somehow sprang up from the heavy floor that she had to walk across to reach the table. Once she sat down, the young lady's glazed eyes and fixed smile confirmed Mara's fears.

After the men left for the field, Mara remained seated for longer than usual, but Emily didn't notice as her mind was elsewhere.

'You haven't touched any breakfast,' Mara said, pointing to the few slices of toast left on a plate.

At last, Emily looked at her mother and shook her head. 'I'm not at all hungry, Ma. Leave it there, and I'll have some later this morning.'

'How can you not be hungry, girl? You barely ate any dinner last night.'

'But it was cold. You know I can't bear cold meat.'

'Yes, mine was cold too because I couldn't eat a thing while you were missing in that storm. When you finally came back, you were soaked to the bone, and all the hot water we had was needed to bathe your foot.'

Her foot! She hadn't noticed the pain until her mother's reminder of how she'd limped into the farmhouse the previous evening. Glancing down at the floor, she surveyed the ugly swollen foot that now began to throb all over. Her shoe wouldn't fit even if she had remembered to put it on.

'Tell me again about the man who brought you home,' Mara said, in a tone that suggested scepticism.

Feeling the blood rushing into her cheeks, Emily quickly picked up a slice of toast and nibbled the crust while she tried to remember her story. 'I can't tell you much because I didn't look at his face.'

'Oh! Well, that was very irresponsible of you Emily. He could have been some rogue driving around in search of a victim.'

'Well, what should I have done? It took me hours to walk as far as I did. I would still be walking if I had not accepted his offer.'

'No, because Sam and your father went looking for you long before that. They tracked your usual journey as far as the meadow, but there was no sign of you. I can't imagine how you made it back to the road.'

Emily knew her mother was watching her closely meaning she didn't believe her. Suddenly, she could bear the deceit no longer.

'I'm sorry Ma, but I have not been completely honest with you. I know the driver well. It was James Murdoch and ... and ... he has asked me to marry him.' She took a deep breath and then exhaled the anxiety which had been building inside her.

Mara also inhaled deeply, but the breath remained inside her for a seemingly impossible time. Finally, shaking her head, she said, 'You silly girl. What have you done?'

It was not the reaction Emily had hoped for but she appreciated the shock she had given her mother who was still shaking her head. 'Please, don't be angry. We have been in love for months and can bear to be apart no longer.'

'And where do you intend to be together?' Mara asked. Her tone was still harsh. 'There is little room here so you will need to move into the manor, and I cannot see his father welcoming you.'

'We will move to Oxford while he completes his law studies. Then we will move back to start a family.'

'Don't be a fool!' Mara snapped. 'And I wouldn't say such nonsense to your father. He will drop dead with the shock.'

At first, Emily was stunned into silence by her mother's anger but gradually felt her own anger brewing. 'I thought you of all people would understand. You gave up everything to be with Pa and say you've never regretted it. How was that any different from us?'

'I'll tell you how it was different. Because we were of the same sort of people. That man is not meant for you. He won't marry you, whatever he said. He is only trying to get his wicked way with you.'

Emily fought back the tears as she listened to her mother's chastising. She dreaded where the conversation was heading and decided to withdraw from it. 'So, I'm a fool for believing him when he said he loved me. We shall leave it at that.'

Mara reached across the table and grabbed Emily's hands in hers. 'I have little doubt that he loves you. What man could not? But love is rarely enough in this world. The rich marry within their circle and the poor within theirs. It has always been that way and will be forevermore — for him too.'

Snatching her hands back, Emily got to her feet and, ignoring the searing pain in her foot, limped towards the door.

'You haven't got your shoes on,' Mara called after her.

Emily did not answer. She would remain barefooted that day.

***

James stared at the study door with his fisted hand hanging in mid-air. He couldn't yet bring himself to complete the act of knocking. But before he had a chance to walk away, the door opened and his father stood opposite him.

'What in the blazes are you doing just standing there, man? Is there nothing more productive you could be doing?'

'No, Sir. I have come to speak with you.' James spat the words out so quickly, he wasn't sure if he had actually said them out loud. But he had.

'Well, come in then. I have not got all day,' Charles said, without a hint of irony before turning around and walking to the window.

James followed his father back into the library. He sat down before waiting to be asked as his legs felt like jelly.

'I have something to tell you, Father. It is regarding Miss Fortesque.'

'Do not tell me you have put her in the family way.'

'No, of course not. It is just, well —'

'What is it? Spit it out, man!'

'I have been thinking about this for a while and ... it needs to be said that ... I am not going to marry her, Father.'

For a few seconds, Charles' expression remained fixed as if he was interpreting the jumble of words his son had spoken. Then, banging his forehead with one palm, he walked over to the cabinet and poured two drinks. Slamming one glass down on the table in front of James, he gulped down the contents of the second. At last, he spoke, his voice surprisingly gentle.

'Look, Son, I understand how you feel. You are young, just out of college, and want to live a little before settling down. Nobody is going to stop you. The engagement can last for a year or two.'

'I am not getting engaged either, at least not to Arabella.'

'Oh, I see. She has said no, I take it. Well, it will have to be Letitia.'

'No. I am making my own choice.'

Charles raised his eyebrows. 'What is that supposed to mean?' His voice had regained its usual sharp tone.

'It is my intention to marry Emily Mayer.'

His father laughed. 'Mayer? You do not mean the farmer's daughter, I hope.'

'Yes, I do. Is it so strange?'

He strode over to James and bawled into his face. 'Is this some kind of joke? Have you lost your mind?'

'What difference does it make to you who I marry? I do not care about titles or wealth so you should not either.'

For a short while, James wasn't sure whether his father would strike him and wondered what he would do in response. But there was no physical assault. Rather, Charles regained his composure and sat down behind his desk.

'You are right about one thing at least. You are far too immature to marry anyone. I should have known better than to expect more from a spoilt boy who has spent most of his life in school. Well, there is a lot for you to learn and I shall start by teaching you what is what. You can marry whoever you want but do not expect anything from me.'

'That is fine. I shall return to Oxford and study the bar so I can support myself and my wife.'

'And where will your wife live while you are back in the classroom?'

'She will stay with her family, of course.'

'They will be in the workhouse by the time you come back.'

'What do you mean?'

'The lease on the farm is ending soon. Do you honestly think I will renew it if you carry out your threat?'

'That is outrageous. You cannot do that.'

'Why not? The farm is barely making money. There are far better uses for that land and those people are in the way.'

'They have rights.' James was shaking his head in disbelief.

Charles laughed. 'You really should study law because you have no idea what I can do with my own land. We shall see if your farmer wench still wants you when you are a pauper.'

James was at a dead end. He knew his father well enough to realise he cared nothing about the workers on his land. Emily's parents would be homeless and without a source of income. Would she want that even if it meant they could be together? His father's words cut like a knife because they were not far-fetched. Maybe Emily wasn't even sure herself as she had only known him as the squire's son and heir of all his estate. It wasn't fair to assume that she would want him at all costs. Her father was getting older and might struggle to find other work.

Sensing he was winning, Charles changed his tone. 'Listen, son. Why not go away for a while and consider your options? Neither of us should rush into decisions that cannot be undone. And there is the ball tonight and that is no place for such serious matters.'

After getting to his feet, James walked out of the library with his head down.

***

Lilly rushed up the red-carpeted steps careful not to trip on the mass of petticoats she carried in both arms. Although unable to see one foot in front of the other, she knew every inch of every tread which made up the grand sweeping staircase. She had been up and down them enough times. Much had changed since the early days when she was restricted to the servants' stairs and she only went as far as the first floor to empty chamber pots. Besides an increase in wages, her promotion to lady's maid brought other benefits. One such honour was the right to be visible in the presence of passing lords and ladies without the need to duck behind doors or curtains to protect their delicate senses. Who knew what position she could aspire to if she stayed another twelve years? But Lilly did not intend to become the next housekeeper even if Miss Howells were to marry and leave, something no one imagined happening.

With her face still buried in cotton and lace, Lilly entered the bedroom of Arabella Fortesque who was sitting at her dressing table. Lilly dropped the bundle of undergarments on a couch and took up her position behind her mistress.

'I do not think I shall wear the Allard, Lilly. It makes me look fat.'

'Now that is impossible, Miss. No dress could do such a thing.'

Arabella held up a necklace in each hand. 'Should I go for the ruby or the emerald?'

'The emerald will match your eyes, Miss. Tell me if this pulls,' Lilly said while brushing the glossy locks of hair in front of her.

'Oh, do what you will,' Arabella said, waving her hand. 'I want to look my best whatever pain I must suffer.'

'Are there any gentlemen you hope to see in particular, miss?' Lilly asked while parting the hair ready for plaiting. 'Mrs Mallard said that there are many guests invited.'

'Only one, Lilly. There is only one gentleman that I care about and all the others can go hang.'

'And who might that be, Miss?'

'Well, it is a secret and you must not dare tell anyone, Lilly, but his name is James Murdoch. He has recently returned from Oxford and is heir to the Murdoch estate.'

'Is he handsome, Miss? I don't believe I've seen him.'

'Oh my! James is the most handsome man anyone has ever seen. He is tall and dark and has eyes so black they reflect the stars.'

'He sounds very dashing, Miss but he will be lucky to have you.'

'Oh, but it is not without difficulty. Mama and Papa disapprove. They say he is a drunken lout. They would rather have me marry some old army major or wizened earl.'

'Nearly finished.'

'There is Douglas, but he is most certainly not ready to marry and Lettie has a weakness for him. Lilly, I do not think I shall wear either of these. They make me look like an old duchess. And they would distract James' eyes from my slender neck.' She put down the jewelled necklaces and picked up a gold pendant with encrusted diamonds. 'This one will do just fine. No one will notice it.'

Lilly finished pinning up the plaits just as the door burst open and Letitia Harding rushed into the bedroom.

'I am so excited, Belle. How long until people start to arrive? The boys will not be here until later so we must keep ourselves perfectly pretty.' Letitia flung herself onto the bed before glancing at Lilly who, understanding the message behind the look, immediately left the room.

Lilly used the servants' stairs to return to the kitchen. She had no desire to rub shoulders with any more arriving guests who would be sure to think of something she could do for them — especially the male ones.

***

'I am not going to spend the rest of my life with a woman I do not love,' James said, picking up the wooden cue balanced on his knees. Putting too much force on the end of the cue, he swore silently as the red ball rebounded off the corner hole and rolled back to him. 'What difference does it make to the old man who I marry? We would not be spending any time with him.'

Douglas took a sip of whiskey before taking his turn at the billiard table. He was still absorbing the bombshell news that his friend had given him several minutes earlier — that he planned to marry the daughter of a poor farmer.

'I say, you are being rather mean about the lovely Miss Fortesque She is a dash pretty girl and worthy of far better men than you, old bean.' He placed his cue on the table and hit the red ball into the same pocket James had missed seconds earlier. 'I would marry her myself in a jiffy if I was not going on military duty, and, of course, for the fact that she is besotted with you. No doubt she will be looking spectacular later on this evening.'

'She is very pretty and fun to be with but ...' he trailed off not caring to talk about anyone but Emily.

'But what? You are not making much sense.'

'I cannot explain what it was like when I first saw Emily. There was no doubt in my mind that she was the one and there would never be anyone in the world who could compete with her. Every time I close my eyes I see her standing there, a porcelain doll illuminating the darkness. She has lit up my life. I do not think I was alive before we met, just existing.'

'Oh heavens above. Would you listen to yourself? Life is not a poem, James. It is filled with responsibility and family commitments which should come before self-gratification.'

'You think I am selfish for wanting to marry the one I love. Surely there are worse things I could do. And I still do not see why you are against it, Douglas. You are supposed to be my best friend.'

'And as your best friend, I am giving you advice. How much time have you spent with this girl? You do not know anything about her or her family for that matter.'

James pummelled another missed shot before draining his whiskey glass. 'Where is that damn bottle? There it is.'

He sat down and topped up his glass. 'I intend to marry her, not her family about whom I could not care less. They matter not.'

'But they do matter, James. She is not just their daughter; she works for them. If you take her away, they will have to find someone to replace her. She may be a pretty dairymaid, but she is their only dairymaid. Perhaps she will not want to leave them. After all, nineteen is young to be married and taken away from the life you have always known.'

Although batting away most of his friend's efforts to dissuade him, James found Douglas' last words filtering through his mental defence. Emily loved her life in the village. When he'd mentioned his plans for them to live in Oxford while he trained as a lawyer, she was less than enthusiastic.

'What about your father? Is there any hope of bringing him on side?'

'Not right now,' James replied. 'He has threatened to cut me off from the estate. Although, I cannot imagine who else he would leave it to.'

'And what does the lovely Emily make of that?' Douglas said. 'She would be giving up everything merely to marry a pauper. Can you be certain that she is not a little attracted to you because of who your father is rather than who you are?'

'No. She loves me. I can see it in her eyes, her lovely blue eyes.'

'She loves James Murdoch who happens to be the heir to the Murdoch estate. Will she love James Murdoch the poor struggling lawyer? I recommend you hold off on the marriage until she gets used to you as simple James Murdoch.

James remained silent while desperately searching his mind for a response to his friend's recommendation. There was no doubt that he was correct in what he said. Emily had only known him as the son of a rich man, who spent his leisure in aristocratic circles. Even she could not know the answer to Douglas' question. As he battled with the doubts in his head, the image of his mother came to him. She had given up so much to marry his father, her homeland, her family, and her social position, yet their love had not survived long past his birth. Theirs was a poor example of marrying for love.

'Dammit! Why do families have to be so complicated? You are lucky to be escaping from yours.'

Douglas laughed. 'Well, I do not intend for my absence to be permanent but it will be a chance to be myself, even if only for a short while. As I suggested before, you should join me. It would be good for you to clear your head.'

'That is what my father said, amongst other things.' James' expression grew dark.

'What other things?'

'He will throw the Mayer family off the farm if I marry Emily.'

'Good grief! Well, that settles it as far as I am concerned. You must not make any hasty decisions, apart from coming with me. My father knows the Brigadier well so there would be no problem with you being accepted.'

'But what could I tell Emily? I promised that we would leave for Oxford before Christmas.'

'Before Christmas? That gives you more than enough time. Come to Scotland and by the time we come back, things may well have settled. What do you say?'

James could feel his head starting to throb so he poured himself another whiskey. At that moment the idea of being away from the situation was appealing even if it was only as far as Scotland.

'Alright. I shall think about it,' he said. He picked up his cue and took a shot at a green ball. It went into the furthest pocket.

Chapter Eleven

The courtyard at Bamley Hall was a scene of such splendour and elegance that even the horses seemed hypnotised by their blinkered view. Dozens of ball gowns weaved between each other and the numerous assembled carriages. The pale and unassuming colours of the expensive fabrics were offset by the elaborate trimmings of bows, ribbons and buckles as well as skirt circumferences of up to six yards.

Inside the hall, Arabella was naturally the centre of attention as the ball was in her honour. Lord and Lady Fortesque had invited several eligible and suitable men though they suspected her choice was limited to two, both of whom had yet to arrive. Neither parent shared their daughter's preferences whom they felt were too immature in age and character. For Arabella, they wanted a sensible husband who would offer her a safe and stable marriage. In their opinion, neither of their daughter's choices matched that description.

Two hours later, James and Douglas, already drunk, turned up in a hackney carriage. After entering the main hall, Douglas made straight for Lilly who was standing silently while holding a tray of champagne flutes. Her eyes were fixed on a point above the doorway as the servants were not allowed to make eye contact with the guests.

Taking a large sip from the glass, Douglas spat out the champagne. 'Blast, this is as flat as ditchwater.'

Lilly did not reply nor attempt to wipe the champagne from her sleeve. Instead, she took the tray back to the kitchen and then, using the servants' staircase, made her way to Arabella's bedroom. She would spend the remainder of the evening by herself. There was enough to do sorting out the dresses piled high on the bed, a tedious job but preferable to being treated like dirt by conceited guests. For every rejected gown, there was a petticoat, bodice and crinoline beside dozens of pairs of shoes and stockings. However, no sooner had she picked up the top garment than the door flung open and Arabella rushed in.

'Oh, Lilly. Thank goodness! James has just arrived and I need you to tidy my hair. It looks a mess.'

'Certainly, Miss.' Lilly put down the bodice she was folding and took her place at the dressing table.

As Lilly pinned back the loose strands, she reluctantly listened to her mistress talking about the goings on below, but mostly about the excitement she felt when word reached her of James' arrival.

'I should be annoyed that he arrived so ... well, of course, I was annoyed but then he asked me to dance and all I could think of was how handsome he looked. Do you not think he is the best-looking man here?'

'I'm not sure I've seen him, Miss.' She did not remind her mistress that it was not her place to look at the arriving men, not that she wished to.

'You must have. He was the last to arrive. Tall with dark hair and he was squiffy but that is what young men are like, would you agree?'

'If you say so, Miss,' Lilly replied, glancing at the reflection of her stained sleeve in the gilded mirror

'Well, I am asking you what you think, Lilly.'

'I don't know many young men, Miss so I could not say one way or the other.'

'Something tells me you do not approve,' Arabella laughed. 'Oh, I suppose you are right, but James will change as soon as we are married. Now, that is enough, Lilly. I shall return.'

'Wait, Miss,' Lilly said, noticing something glinting in Arabella's neckline. She pulled off the gold chain which had wrapped itself around several beads in the bodice. 'This has come undone. Shall I get you another one? You don't want to lose it.' She threaded the diamond pendant back through the chain and reached towards the jewellery box.

'Do not worry,' Arabella said, grabbing the necklace and reclasping the chain herself. 'I do not have time to choose another one.' She exited the room as quickly as she'd entered.

An hour passed by the time Lilly had cleared the bed, and she turned to start on the dressing table cluttered with bows, ribbons, perfume bottles and pots of cream. After dabbing herself with her favourite perfume, she smeared cream over her body, something she did in stages so as not to be caught in the act. Arabella's cosmetics were so expensive that Lilly thought she must now be wearing more than her wages in cream and perfume. Finally, when she could find nothing more to tidy, Lilly decided to return to her duties downstairs.

As she was opening the door, it jammed preventing her from squeezing through the gap. Getting down on her knees, she pushed her fingers between the door and the carpet until finding the obstruction — the pendant. Luckily, the gold and diamonds were unscathed, but the chain was nowhere to be seen. Lilly slipped the pendant into her pocket and, after closing the door, scanned the landing floor for the missing chain. The flecks of orange and yellow in the patterned carpet made it almost impossible to detect the gold chain, so she got down on her hands and knees to crawl inch by inch along the long corridor.

As she reached the midpoint between the door and the stairs, her hand brushed against something cold. It was the chain. After putting it into her pocket alongside the pendant, she was about to stand up when the light around her dimmed. Looking up, she saw her way was blocked by someone's legs. The quality of the black trousers told her the legs belonged to a male guest. Before she had a chance to get to her feet, the nearest candle went out placing the corridor in near darkness.

'Oh dear,' a man said. 'Let me help you.'

Lilly felt two hands go under her arms and, with no time to respond, was whisked to her feet. 'You smell very nice,' he said, pulling her wrist to his nose. 'Hey, I recognise that perfume. Have you been taking stuff that doesn't belong to you?'

'No,' she said defensively. 'I've been clearing up the dressing table. That is why there is perfume on my clothes.'

In the dim light, she could just make out his teeth bared in a wide grin.

'Don't worry. I won't tell if you give me a little kiss.'

'I'm grateful to you for helping me up, Sir, but if you would now be so kind as to let me go. I need to carry out my duties downstairs,' Lilly said in a calm voice.'

This wasn't the first time she had had to fend off a drunk and amorous aristocrat. Her usual tactic was to gradually raise her voice in the hope that one of the other servants would come to her rescue. But the orchestral music from below ruled out that particular escape route. Therefore, she tried to wriggle herself free, but it was proving hopeless.

'Sir, please don't,' Lilly managed to say before his mouth covered hers.

She tried to push him away, but he was holding her so tightly to his body, there was little room to move. As she felt the situation getting out of hand, Lilly struggled more ripping his breast pocket. The man appeared not to notice and began moving his hand up her body. Realising how far the man was intending to go, she lifted her knee towards his groin. He didn't make a sound when, with his face scrunched up, he crumpled to the floor. By the time he opened his streaming eyes, she was gone.

***

Worries over the lease dominated the conversation at the Mayer's dinner table. The months had passed, and there was still no definitive word from Charles Murdoch regarding the length of any renewal, presuming it was extended at all. John Mayer said less than usual allowing his son's point of view to be heard almost unchecked. As Sam's self-assurance increased, so did his father's feeling of dejection.

Mara watched on helplessly as the two men in her family hoped for opposite outcomes, feeling that it was her husband who would eventually lose the battle. She would not disclose to him her conversation with Emily as that might be too much for him to bear. Not that she feared her daughter would be leaving the farm anytime soon and certainly not with the Murdoch lad. If only he would go back to Oxford or London immediately. Emily would think her heart was forever broken, but she would recover soon enough. She would have to.

Emily knew there was much talking going on around her but was unable to decipher the conversation; although, it was not because her mind was elsewhere. Rather, the words seemed far away and muffled as though her ears were blocked with wool and an invisible wall encompassed her. She was aware of the spoon in her hand but somehow could not muster the strength to dip it into the adjacent bowl of beef broth. The longer dinner went on, the stranger the room felt. But then she realised it was not the room which felt strange, but her. Around her, the voices became nearer and the comments briefer until stopping altogether. Next, she found herself rising from her seat and floating across the kitchen.

Within hours, Emily was lying in bed tossing and turning in a state of semiconsciousness, her muddled mind filled with distorted visions. Several images of James moved around her in circles with expressions changing from sad to happy to angry. One head would move towards her before covering her mouth with his until she was no longer able to breathe. She would fight off each one and then stagger through the meadow with water running down her legs. An older man, whom she assumed to be Charles Murdoch, pursued her while waving a walking cane above his head. Having reached the sanctuary of the farmhouse, she would open the door to find her father standing with an axe in his hand and her mother pleading with him and screaming at her. Thankfully, when the terror peaked, Emily would wake to find herself safe in her bedroom with nobody circling or chasing her. But such was her weakness, she could move her eyes and nothing else. Therefore, she would drift back into a disturbed sleep, for the nightmares to begin again.

***

Only Sam and John went to church the next morning, with Mara staying home to nurse Emily who had a fever. When the younger man saw Lilly's nervous eyes, he knew she had something important to tell him. Grasping his hands through the entire service, only one possibility swirled around in his mind. They were always so careful, but sometimes that was not enough. How would Lilly react? Surely it would put an end to their plans to move to London. Sam wouldn't mind so much, but Lilly would be devastated. She would have to move into the farmhouse until they were able to afford their own lodgings. It might take a year or two ... or longer.

Once outside the church, Lilly took hold of Sam's hand and led him into the graveyard where they could speak in private. When he heard what had happened to his girlfriend the previous evening, he could barely conceal his rage and wanted to confront the perpetrator there and then. Lilly pulled him back.

'The last thing I need is for you to get into trouble over this. Besides, he's not even here. I saw his carriage leaving this morning and it was going in the opposite direction. He will be in no fit state for church.'

'Then I'll pay him a visit when I get back. He's not going to get away with this, Lilly.'

'And what good would that do? His father would throw your family off the land and they would be destitute. I cannot bear us to have anything more to do with that man. I never want to see or hear of him again.'

'But you say he is always at the house.'

'Yes, and he is supposed to be getting engaged to Arabella. He's an absolute rat.'

'And you are certain it was him?'

'Not until I saw him this morning as he was leaving. He was bold as brass and not even trying to hide the rip in his jacket.'

'Well, if you continue to work in that place, it can't be anywhere near that woman he's engaged to.'

Lilly's response to that demand was to purse her lips and then take hold of both Sam's hands. 'I'm not going to continue to work there, Sam, at least not after tomorrow.'

'I don't understand,' he said, his mind racing. 'Where are you going? Please don't leave me, Lilly.'

'Hey, don't worry. Adam spoke to a shop owner in London. There is a new milliner opening soon and they want two girls to train straight away. He said they'll keep a position open for me for a few days, but no longer. It's what we've been planning for so long ... just a few months earlier, that's all. You can stay here until sorting out the farm, and I'll come back on the train to see you. But I need to go straight away.'

A few days! Sam could not find the words to respond. For Lilly to train as a milliner would be a big step up from working in a factory. The pay might not be as good to start, but it would improve once she trained. And to work on the shop floor, Lilly would be set up for life. He knew he couldn't deny her the opportunity.

But he would not let her go alone.

***

Chapter Twelve

When Emily first heard the birds singing loudly from outside the window, she assumed it was early morning yet as she listened on, their melodic notes lacked the intensity of the dawn chorus. Surely it was not evening already. How could she have slept through the whole day? Having got to her feet, she immediately fell back onto the bed but, determined not to spend another minute in her bedroom, she wrapped a blanket around herself and forced her jelly-like legs to the door.

When Emily made it downstairs, she was surprised to see Tommy Barker sitting at the table along with both of her parents. A low orange glow still illuminated the western sky therefore her father should still be out in the field utilising every scrap of daylight. She assumed he'd left

Sam to finish up, but that didn't explain his entertaining Tommy, or his glum expression.

'Hello, Tommy,' she said, in an attempt to gauge the mood without asking the reason for his impromptu visit.

'Hello, doll,' he replied with his familiar wink. 'You're looking as though you've died and come back again.'

Baffled by his words, Emily looked at her mother. Mara was chewing her lips as she did when she was nervous. Then, without standing up, she pointed to her chair. 'Sit yourself down, luv. There's enough tea in the pot for you to warm your frozen fingers before I dish out the dinner.'

As Emily sat on the one empty chair, she hit her foot against something soft under the table. Peering down, she noticed a small bulging sack tied at the top with tattered rope.

'Are you leaving?' she said, looking at the young man opposite her. 'I thought you were here until November.'

Tommy didn't reply but instead looked across the table at Emily's father before settling his eyes on Mara. Several sounds followed: the chinking of china; the slurping of tea; the loud swallowing; and small coughs. But no words. It was all that was needed to tell Emily something serious had happened. And whatever that something was would affect her too. Suddenly, her brother's absence from the table grew more significant.

'Where's Sam?' Emily asked, unsure she wanted the answer.

'He's gone, luv,' Mara replied, at last.

Emily gasped. Feeling her heart pounding with fear, she tried to keep calm. 'Please tell me he's not dead.'

Her father's snort was not the response of a bereaved man and came as a huge relief to Emily. It was her mother who gave her the upsetting news.

'Your brother's gone off to London and left us in the lurch.'

'London! But he was here yesterday. Have I just missed him?'

'No, luv. He went two days ago. You've been in bed for three.'

Emily's limp body turned to stone at the reality of the situation. She had lost three days. Three days! The blood rushed through her veins bringing her body back to life.

'What day is it?' she cried in panic.

'Tuesday,' Tommy said with a sympathetic look.

Emily breathed a sigh of relief realising that she had not missed her rendezvous with James. She had a further three days to recover and clean herself up. Returning to the more pressing matter of her brother, she said, 'How could he do such a thing? He knows that we can't manage the farm without him,' she said, trailing off as her eyes fell on Tommy. 'Why are you here?'

He smiled awkwardly, and, after glancing at Mara and John for guidance, explained his presence. 'Sam asked me if I would help out on the farm until you could find a labourer. I'm around for a couple of months so agreed.'

'But the work starts at dawn, and you live so far ...' Emily's glanced down at the sack for a second time then looked back up at Tommy with her eyes stretched wide open. 'Oh my!'

'Tommy will be staying with us while helping out on the farm,' John said. 'It's the least we can offer him as there's no money for pay.'

'He will be sleeping in Sam's room,' Mara said. Then, with a smiling nod at Tommy, continued, 'He's practically family anyway.'

For the remainder of the meal, Emily avoided meeting Tommy's eyes which she knew were, at times observing her reaction to their new situation. She cringed at the thought of sleeping in a bed only a couple of yards away from a man who had been a practical stranger only weeks earlier. Regardless of what her mother said, he was no longer the young lad that she and her brother played with occasionally. He had grown into an adult — and so had she.

***

Sam and Lilly's experience of city life began as soon as they stepped onto the platform at Paddington. Hit by the foul stench, Sam laughingly suggested reembarking the train. After taking a few moments to gather their senses and gripping their bags tightly, they walked further into the thick mist.

The London smog was the first of many new encounters they were to face. From the station to the high streets, there were people everywhere. In all directions, it was impossible to stretch an arm without touching an irate stranger, much to the young couple's amusement. Yet beyond a tut or flinch, nobody reacted; just as they didn't smile, apologise or say good morning. Carriages of every shape and size fought with each other to fill rare gaps in the road, their wheels rumbling like thunder on the urine-soaked cobbles.

The throng of people began to disperse as Sam and Lilly moved further away from the station into the narrow backstreets where long rows of terraced houses fed into others. One property looked like another – two-storey stone fronts with large windows and a narrow door – causing Sam to worry they wouldn't be able to distinguish the house they were looking for. But Lilly had planned the journey meticulously and, memorising the directions, led them straight to their new lodgings.

Sam grimaced as he lifted both bags onto the single bed that took up half the room. It would be impossible to tell what the dark mattress stains were unless through smell or taste, and he wasn't about to do either. Even worse, was the solitary blanket provided which clearly had not been washed for several months at least. Turning to Lilly, he shook his head. 'This is not how I pictured the start of our life together,' he said sadly.

Lilly grabbed his hands and smiled. 'It's only for a few days until we have had a chance to look around. Think of it as an adventure.'

His eyes glinted at the word. 'Not so much for me but, my love, it will be an adventure for you who has never used an outside water closet.'

Nudging him with her elbows, she tutted. 'That is not true, and you know it. Anyway, if that is the hardest thing we face, I think we will be just fine here.'

***

Despite being desperate to get back to work, Emily was not allowed out of the house the following day. Mara said she could manage the dairy duties for a few more days while her daughter fully recovered. Emily's insistent protests grew louder and more frantic as Friday got closer until on Thursday evening, she declared that she would return to her duties the following morning. Her father nodded in agreement.

'Well, I must say you look better than before you were ill,' he said. 'What do you say, lad?'

Tommy visibly squirmed at the question. 'Er, yes, Mr Mayer,' he mumbled as his face turned pink. 'I would say your daughter always looks well to me.'

At those words, the older couple glanced at each other in mutual satisfaction. Oblivious to the varying emotions of the others at the table, Emily's mind raced forward to the following afternoon's plan. She would have to go to the meadow between milkings as her mother would be sure to stop her going in the dimming light. There would still be time to change into her best dress even though she believed James didn't mind what clothes she wore. He loved her as much as she loved him, and the only clothes that mattered were those they would wear on their wedding day. A tingle ran down her spine at the thought of marrying him. She almost squealed with delight before remembering she was in company.

'I'm not so sure,' Mara said. 'Another couple of days rest won't do her any harm.

Hearing her mother's words, Emily focussed on sounding well enough to reassure her. In an upbeat voice, she said, 'Do we know where Sam and Lilly live now? I want to write to them so they can describe life in London.'

John tutted. 'We don't know where they are. They could be sleeping under a bridge.'

'A bridge? Surely, they had jobs and somewhere to live arranged before they left. Lilly's been planning this move for as long as we've known her.'

When universal silence was the only response to Emily's comments, she began to sense there was something she had yet to find out — something bad. She glanced at Tommy, but he was keeping his eyes firmly fixed on his plate; Mara mirrored his actions. It was John Mayer who, still seething from his son's departure, began to fill in his daughter.

'I always said that girl was too big for her boots. It's a wonder she lasted as long as she did without getting sacked.'

'Lilly's been sacked? I don't believe it.'

'And you'd be right not to,' Mara said, glaring at her husband. 'Lilly left the job of her own accord. It's just a pity there was no notice for us.'

'Left us in the lurch, they did,' John said. He quickly added, 'With much respect to you, lad.'

Tommy merely nodded not wishing to involve himself in such family matters. However, Emily guessed he knew a great deal more than she did and directed her next question to him.

'You said my brother asked you to take over before he left, Tommy. Is that correct?'

'Aye, he did and I had nought going on so was happy to oblige.'

'Did he tell you what happened with Lilly?'

'A ruckus of sorts during some fancy ball. One of the guests tried to force himself on her, but she managed to fight him off. It shook her up badly.'

'That's terrible. Poor Lilly. Is she alright?'

John laughed. 'Don't concern yourself, luv. I'm sure she gave as good as she got. He picked on the wrong servant girl.'

'Did she tell the Fortesques?' Emily asked. 'She mentioned to me that they have been quite good to her. And the daughter, Arabella? Surely, she told her.'

'Lilly didn't bother. She said Arabella's too wrapped up in her fiancé to be interested in her problems.'

Fiancé. It could not be. Emily dared not ask until she could bear it no longer. 'Who is her fiancé?'

'That's enough of this talk,' Mara said. She stood up to signal the end of the meal. 'Pass me the dishes, Emily, luv.'

Noticing the panic in her mother's voice, Emily felt her own building up inside of her. While trying to sound calm, she repeated her question to Tommy. He answered.

'James Murdoch.'

***

The final light of day tinted the sky above James as he entered the meadow. He should have been concerned for the safety of a young woman wandering alone in such dimness, and of course he was. However, he knew Emily would be there regardless of their planned meeting. Therefore, he rushed to the spot where he had first set eyes on her, where the wild grass was flatter, worn down by human feet. In his mind's eye, he could see her strolling aimlessly through the brittle overgrowth with her palms bouncing off the shrivelled seeds which had failed to blow into another existence.

She'd taught him everything he knew about the circle of nature as there had been no room for such trivial knowledge in his education. Before meeting Emily, his world was comprised only of past existences, long dead but kept alive by the universities and elite professions to set them apart from the common man. The gentry did not need to distinguish between a birch and a beech, a hawk and a kestrel, or a salmon and a trout. Other life forms were immaterial when one had servants to tend, prepare and serve them. Even hunting held little interest for James, though not for any moral or squeamish reasons. Rather, he saw little point in chasing vermin around the countryside. That was where he and Douglas differed. His friend viewed hunting as the sport of kings, far more invigorating than any drug offered at the many dubious parties they both attended. At least Douglas could not do as much damage as he was wont to do while under the influence of those drugs, apart from to the poor wretched fox, of course.

From somewhere nearby, the sweet singing of a blackbird brought James' thoughts back to Emily. He realised it was getting late for her to come especially as they had arranged to meet before dusk. Perhaps her foot was still hurting yet it had seemed fine when he'd dropped her off outside the cottage. A worrying possibility came to mind as he continued to visualise her walking through the front door. Had she told her parents about their intentions? They had agreed it best to wait for him to prepare lodgings after Christmas but they may have seen his carriage and guessed he and Emily had been together. He wondered if her father would react any more positively than James' own father had. Perhaps not. The former would be well aware of the vindictive nature of his landlord.

The birdsong was more frantic now drawing James' attention to its source — a male blackbird standing on a bare tree branch. It was the same tree Emily used to deposit excess food which had not been eaten. Was the blackbird wondering where she was too? James continued to watch until all that was visible were dark streaks and shadows and a tiny shape from which the singing continued.

From its unknown hiding place, the moon emerged casting a silver sheen over the musical scene and creating a fairytale image. James strolled up to the tree causing the blackbird to fly away. He knew it was time for him to leave too. Emily wasn't going to be there.

Reaching into his pocket, he pulled out a black velvet box and placed it in the tree hollow.

Then he went home to pack.

Chapter Thirteen

Tommy cursed as the watery liquid splashed over his shoes for the umpteenth time. There would be hell to pay if Mara found out how much milk had been lost due to his heavy-handedness. It beggared belief that a slip of a lass like Emily could carry such heavy buckets at all, let alone without spilling a drop. In fact, everything about Emily impressed him so much that he believed there was no other girl like her the world over. Before moving into the farmhouse, he'd regarded her as the farmer's daughter or Sam's sister as there was no need to consider her as an individual. Over the last few weeks, the formalities and inhibitions had fallen away leaving the young man and woman the closest of friends.

For Emily, he knew that was as far as it went because she was just too natural with him, too much at ease. If she only knew how his heart longed for her cheeks to blush, or for her to smile shyly rather than laugh out loud. How would she react if she knew how he really felt? She might insist he left the farmhouse, keep to his plan and embark on the next ship to Australia, the one which was due to sail in a couple of months. He hadn't told her that he was considering delaying his departure as the Mayers had asked him to stay on at the farm for a while longer. There had been no interest in the vacancy he'd filled temporarily which was hardly a surprise given the lack of security. With the lease coming to an end, and still no word from the squire, no one else was fool enough to commit to what was essentially working for board and lodge for possibly only a few months. It was fine for Tommy as ships came and went all the time and he would always get a place onboard. For other workers, it was a different story.

Sam was right to move on. There was no future for him and Lilly in the countryside. Even if the lease was extended, Sam told him Lilly would never move into the farmhouse. And Sam would never give up Lilly.

***

The sky was still dark when Sam left for his factory shift although it was difficult to tell given the smog outside. If that wasn't bad enough, the narrow streets and high buildings blocked out any sight of the sky from inside their tiny bedsit. As she did every morning, Lilly tried her best to perfect her hair while using the meagre light given off by a thin candle resting on the window sill. There was no room for a second candle even if they could have afforded one. Sam did not consider good lighting a priority, especially in winter when they were both at work during each short day. After she placed the last pin in her hat, Lilly blew out the solitary candle and walked out of the room and down the stairs. In the hallway, she met the landlady.

'Morning Mrs Murphy,' Lilly said, as she passed the thin middle-aged woman. 'I'm going to work.'

'Must be some fancy job you got,' Mrs Murphy said, looking Lilly up and down. '

Lilly smiled awkwardly. 'It's just an apprenticeship, but I hope it leads to something better.'

'Well, you've got your husband's money for now, so you got yourself a nice little earner between you.'

'Oh, hardly, Mrs Murphy. I'm on next to nothing until I finish my apprenticeship, and then I'll start on the lowest wage for a milliner. I was hoping to work some hours in the shop, but my clothes are far too tatty for the West End.' She raised her skirt a few inches to show the worn hemline.

'Why ever don't you get that man of yours to buy you a new frock then? It'll be worth the investment.'

'Unfortunately, after he's paid for our food and rent, there's very little to spare. And I'd need a decent dress if I was to work in the shop.'

'You could pawn your necklace for a pretty penny.'

Lilly blushed and instinctively felt for the gold chain hidden under her high collar. Mrs Murphy must have had eyes like a hawk to notice it.

'Oh, I don't think so. It is very special to me.'

'I bet it is too. Well, if you change your mind, there's a shop at the corner of Andover Street what'll give you something for it. Though I can't say if it'll be a fair price. Anyhow, I gotta be getting on with this cleaning,' she said, before disappearing through a worm-ridden wooden door.

Ten minutes later, Lilly happened to come by the shop mentioned by her landlady. It was hardly a surprise to find it small, shabby and very much like she imagined a pawn-broker to be. Knowing Arabella's necklace would have cost more than most people could afford, Lilly was sure it would be out of place among weathered brass pocket watches and enamel brooches, She tried peering through the dirty panes of glass to see the standard of jewellery sold, but all she could make out was a long wooden counter with a tall thin figure behind it. It would be another hour at least before the shop opened, so she continued on her journey to work.

The thought of selling the necklace had never crossed Lilly's mind before that morning. They were already in London when she first discovered it in the deep pocket of her skirt, so there was nothing to be done at that time. However, she was an honest person and planned to give it to Adam the next time she saw him. Not wanting to leave it lying around the bedsit, she put it in the safest place she could think of — around her neck. Until that morning, Sam had been the only other person who knew about the necklace and its probable value. Suddenly, Mrs Murphy was aware of it too, and who knew how many people she might tell. Lilly would no longer feel comfortable walking through the dark narrow streets of London. Perhaps she would call in the shop on her way back home.

***

James stared at the stag standing motionless only yards from his window, its magnificent antlers a crown far greater than any king's. The stag moved at last, and James could return his attention to the four walls around him. He had never felt so bored in all his life. Although appreciating the rugged beauty of the Scottish Highlands, he had seen enough of lochs, dales and mountains and yearned for the flat greenery of Oxfordshire and Gloucestershire — and Emily.

'Here is another letter for you,' said Douglas. He had just entered their room. 'It is the third this week so the poor girl is really missing you.'

Another pang of disappointment pierced James' skin. Of course, it wasn't from Emily because she had no idea where he was. He'd left before telling her. If only she'd kept to their arrangement. The thought had crossed his mind that she'd gone earlier in the day. If so, it was not the end of the world. There was only another week before he and Douglas left the training camp albeit for different destinations. They had been in three weeks when news began trickling in from the Black Sea. Although James agreed to join Douglas in Scotland, he merely had a strenuous holiday in mind. It was also a way to placate his father who wanted James to spend some time away to consider his options. Well, he had done that and nothing had changed. He would soon be back in Gloucester.

In contrast, Douglas was keen to join his compatriots fighting Russia in the Black Sea. The conflict, which had been going on for a year, held little interest for James until the scene of battle had moved to Crimea. He'd studied a great deal about the peninsula where the ancient Greeks had established colonies, and it had become a far-flung place of fascination for him. If circumstances were different, he would probably be happy to enlist as so many men of his class had done. And maybe he would. But not before he and Emily were married and settled.

'Well?' Douglas grinned. He glanced at the still unopened letter in James' hand.

James opened the envelope and took out the scented paper he had no desire to read. However, there was little else to do until dinner. He looked down at the delicately beautiful handwriting and skimmed the first few lines until he reached a familiar but out-of-place name – Mayer. Rereading the letter, his curiosity was satisfied. Arabella's long-serving dressmaid had abandoned her, running off with the son of a tenant farmer called Mayer.

'Is anything wrong?' Douglas asked, reading his friend's confused expression.

'Not really. Except Arabella is upset because her maid has left. Surely, she can get another.'

'Is that it? Does she say anything else? I must say you are looking rather pensive.'

'Er, well she mentions Emily's brother with whom the maid has left. Hold on while I finish this. No, that is about it.' He glanced up in time to see his friend's worried face. 'What is the matter? Did you know about this?'

Douglas shrugged his shoulders. 'Letty mentioned something about it in her last letter.'

'I do not understand what the issue is. Surely servants leave and have to be replaced occasionally.'

'Well, apparently this servant did not leave empty-handed. She took a rather expensive piece of jewellery with her.'

'Gosh! What the blazes does she expect to do with that? She will not be able to sell it to decent jewellers.'

'There are certain to be takers in London. That is where the filthy thieves have made for.'

'Hold on. So, Mayer's son has gone with her. The father will have a difficult time managing the farm with just his wife and Emily there.'

'Not as I have heard,' Douglas said.

'What are you talking about? Surely, it would be impossible to hire a countryside labourer these days. It will be the end of the farm. Perhaps it is for the best. Emily will be of little use to them. A strong man is needed.'

'There is a replacement already. A fine specimen of a man too if I must say so. Looks the sort who has been away for a good while — fair-haired, tanned.'

James' mouth dropped. The image of Emily at the fair with the blond man came to his mind. At that time, seeing them together had tortured his soul. James could not bear the idea that they were so close again.

'And I suppose Lettie mentioned that in her letter,' James said.

'As a matter of fact, she did.'

'And how would dear Lettie know the goings on of a small farm?'

'Apparently, your father mentioned it while dining with the Hardings.'

James cursed his father under his breath. 'Well, whoever this man is, he will be going away again soon. I cannot imagine there would be any money in the job.'

Douglas shook his head. 'Maybe not. He has moved into the farmhouse, so will have his board and lodge given to him.'

'What sort of a job is that for "a fine specimen of a man",' James said. 'He sounds more like a beggar.'

'Come off it, James. He is obviously after more than a free bowl of broth. If he has moved in, I would say he already has it. Look, forget all that. It is time you replied to Bella.

James gazed at the crumpled paper he had allowed to drop to the floor. He picked up a pen and notepad.

***

Emily watched Tommy as he came into the house and wiped his muddy boots on the straw mat by the door. For the past two weeks, he had been doing most of the work on the farm, yet he still had a smile on his face and a spring in his step. It was easy to picture him on a deck, surrounded by shipmates pulling ropes and climbing masts as they raced through the wild seas. It was where he should be before Christmas, but she knew that her parents were doing their utmost to keep him on dry land. He was yet to decide. The postponement of his leaving would be a blessing for her parents and Emily as there was no possibility of them managing without an extra pair of hands. And Tommy had very capable hands; safe hands.

Of course, Emily could not help but think of the fortune teller's prediction that she would have a choice of two paths, one safer than the other. The possibility of Tommy being with her on that safe path filled her with conflicting emotions which both surprised and confused her. With her heart still in tatters, she feared that he was a convenient distraction, to pick her back up from the pit of misery she'd fallen into. Why fear it? Because she was fond of

Tommy and did not want to hurt him in any way. In other circumstances, she could imagine them being together and both living happily ever after. Yet, despite the pain in her heart, there was still a flicker of hope which kept it fluttering each time she thought of James. After all, James had told her he would never marry Arabella. Yes, Tommy may have misheard the name.

Tommy looked up and winked as though sensing he was in her thoughts. 'How are you feeling, Emmy?' he said.

'Awful when I see you working such long hours on my behalf. I wish you would let me help. Sitting on a stool won't do me any harm.'

'Not with you feeling faint all the time. You need to get some solid food inside you.'

She picked up an apple and bit into it. 'See!'

Tommy smiled. 'Perhaps tomorrow ... for a short while. We'll see how things go.'

Emily glanced at her parents who were oblivious to the conversation, or at least not feeling it necessary to join in. It was almost as though they regarded Tommy as a family member whose opinion counted even when concerning personal matters. Of course, he hadn't exactly been a stranger before as the two families had been close friends for many years. Yet the ease with which he'd settled into Sam's place was quite remarkable. And Emily felt the same. She would certainly miss him when he left ... if he left.

'Don't forget you're taking an urn to Bamley Hall tomorrow,' John said, showing that he had been listening to the conversation.

'I haven't forgotten. Hey, maybe Emmy can come too. It'll make the journey pass by quicker.'

'Oh, I don't know about that. Both of us can't go, Tommy.'

'Yes, you can,' Mara said. 'Getting out of this house will be the best thing for you, even if only for a few hours.'

'Well, if you're sure,' Emily said, before smiling at Tommy. 'It would be nice to have some fresh air.'

'That's settled then,' Tommy replied. 'I'll rise an hour earlier to get a few jobs done before we leave.'

'That's good of you, Tommy,' Mara said, her face glowing. 'I don't know how we ever managed without you.'

Just as an embarrassed Tommy was about to reply with some playful words, they heard the sound of the gate opening outside. All four looked at each other with surprise. They never had visits at such a time unless there was some emergency on the farm. Then there were footsteps getting louder until they were outside the window. Emily's father stood up and walked to the door, steadying himself before he opened it.

'What on earth ...'

'What's the matter?' Mara said, her voice anxious. 'Who is it?'

John stepped back to allow the visitor inside. Sam stood in the doorway shivering his face wracked with pain.

'Lilly's been arrested.'

Chapter Fourteen

Sam sat on the chair vacated by his mother who was frantically trying to prepare some hot food for him. Tommy was also busy organising the small bedroom in a way that would accommodate the two young men. There was no question of anyone leaving the farmhouse at such a late hour so they would have to make do.

Finally, Mara placed some hot bread and dripping in front of her son. 'Get that down you, Sam. You'll feel stronger once you've eaten.'

Despite fearing it would stick in his throat, Sam picked up a slice and took a small bite. He knew his mother well enough not to bother protesting. After swallowing the morsel of bread, he pushed the dish away and banged his fist on the table. 'Damn that man. It's all his fault.'

'Now, now,' his father said sternly. 'There'll be none of that language around this table. You've had a nasty shock and we know you're upset but thumping and cursing will do no good and you know it.'

'I'm sorry,' Sam said, putting his head back in his hands. 'What am I going to do? They could send Lilly to the colonies.'

'What do you mean? They couldn't send her to Africa,' Emily cried. 'Tommy said white people die there.'

Tommy, hearing his name mentioned, shouted down the stairs, 'Nobody gets sent to Africa. It's Australia where they go.'

'Which is the furthest place on earth,' Sam said. 'She might as well be on the moon.'

'Oh, come now,' Mara said. 'They won't send her anywhere when it's her first offence. It's only those who keep getting caught that are transported.'

'It's not her first offence,' Sam snapped. 'Lilly is innocent. She'd forgotten that the necklace was in her pocket and was going to give it back as soon as she got the chance.'

Luckily Sam did not see the exchange of glances between his parents. Emily did and, though sharing their doubts about Lilly's intentions, felt duty-bound to defend her.

'Lilly is as honest as the day is long so, if she said she would return it, I believe her. But, Sam, how did she plan to give it back without returning to the Fortesques' house?'

'She intended to give it to Adam. He's the servant who drives their carriage and said next time he comes to London he'll call in the place where Lilly works. He could have explained that it was an honest mistake, and Lilly never meant to take it with her when she left the house.'

'But what if the pawn shop had sold it? It was such a risk, Sam. That girl has no sense in her painted head,' Mara said, feeling little sympathy for the woman who'd taken her son away. 'And why was it in her pocket to begin with?'

'I told you already, she put it in her pocket when she found it on the floor. Then that brute attacked her. Well, he is going to put things right. That is why I am here.'

There was a loud crashing sound as Mara dropped the iron dish she'd been holding. 'What do you mean "put things right"? I hope you are not thinking of confronting him.'

'That's exactly what I'm going to do. Lilly says he intends to study Law. Well, I can put a stop to that.'

'And what do you propose to do?' John said. 'He's not even here right now. I've heard he's in Scotland.'

'Then I'll speak to his father. I'm not afraid of him. I'll threaten to go to the Law Institution.'

'No one will believe you, son, so there's no point. And you'll only make things worse.'

All the while, Emily remained silent. Every word battered her like a cannonball weakening her further with every hit. Her world was in danger of crashing down around her in full view of her oblivious family. It was only being held up by a single thread of hope — that James was not the man Sam was referring to. He went to Scotland with his friend, Douglas who was sure to have a father of his own. Yes, it had to be Douglas. James would never have attacked a woman because he was a gentleman. And he loved her. At least, he said he did. The sensation of being watched brought her mind back to the present company, and she noticed her mother's eyes were fixed upon her; the worried expression on her mother's face confirmed Emily's worst fear. Muttering some words incomprehensible even to herself, Emily stood up and left the kitchen. Once in the privacy of her bedroom, she collapsed into hysterical sobs.

***

Sam stayed in the farmhouse for one night only, bunking in with Tommy. Despite his mother's pleas for him to remain longer, he insisted on returning to London to be as close as possible to Lilly. Also, he needed to keep his job at the factory to be able to afford the solicitor Tommy mentioned. After much argument, his parents convinced him that confronting the squire could only make things worse for Lilly. Like any father, Charles Murdoch's instincts would be to do everything in his power to protect his son, possibly even using his influence to sign Lilly's transportation order. Only when asked for his opinion did Tommy speak and that was to agree with John and Mara. He also gave Sam the address of a shipowner in London who, he said, owed him a favour. The rich man was sure to know a decent lawyer who might consider taking Lilly's case.

Emily woke up feeling worse than at any time during her fever. She hadn't wanted to close her eyes despite sleep giving her a brief respite from the emotional agony. Waking up would force her to relive the initial shock and devastation. It was already dawn when, overcome with exhaustion, she'd fallen into a cruel dream. She was in the meadow with James. His arms were wrapped tightly around her and their lips touched softly. She could feel his skin, hear his voice, and smell his scent.

How could a dream be so real?

Getting out of bed, she noticed that her foot no longer hurt, not even a twinge. It was as though the whole romance had been in her imagination. She began to blame herself for taking James at his word. He'd told her so many lies, and for what? She was just a challenge to him, a challenge that he'd won. Oh, the shame! Yet mixed up in such negative thoughts were the memories of her encounters with him. She could relive every moment they'd spent together, from the first blurred image of him standing across the meadow to his smile as he drove away after taking her home. If expressions and feelings were anything to go by, there was no doubt in her mind that James wanted to give the impression that he loved her. And some of his words too were impossible to misinterpret — his marriage proposal and plans to take her to Oxford. Why would he be prepared to give up his inheritance if he did not love her? Suddenly, a sinking feeling hit her and she wracked her memory frantically hoping she was mistaken. But no. However he acted, and whatever else he told her, he had never said that he loved her. Was that too much of a lie even for him?

Then another image came to her. It was Lilly pushing a drunken James away. Who was she fooling? James was an arrogant brute who enjoyed playing with lower-status women while all the time he intended to marry within his circle. Anger raced through Emily's body. So many different emotions were exhausting her. She had to pull herself together. With all her remaining mental strength, she cleared her mind of the past few months and got ready to start the day.

***

James and Douglas disembarked the ship stepping into the dark midnight chill of West Crimea. They were among the hundreds of fresh soldiers and volunteers who had another journey in front of them before reaching the battle lines. A guard was waiting for the bedraggled recruits. They followed him out of the port to begin the long trek to the trenches. The recruits were making their way towards the yellow and white streaks peppering the dark blue horizon. The sounds of cannons in the distance became more pronounced with each step they took.

'How long until we reach Sevastopol?' James asked his friend. He dared not mention that his boots were already rubbing his heels. That would make the discomfort more real.

Douglas glanced at his map before shaking his head. 'From what I can make out, we would be lucky to get that far before this war is over.'

'Lucky? You are a braver man than I. To be quite honest, I am feeling rather yellow-bellied at the thought of using this thing.'

'Why James, these things as you call them, are superior weapons which I, for one, am desperate to use. They will blast those muskets into smithereens.'

At that moment, James wished the heavy rifle on his shoulder would turn to smithereens, even if it meant being without the 'superior weapon'. He imagined that carrying it for miles and miles could kill him anyway.

They continued marching over scorched vineyards, before crossing a wooden bridge into a village. Dilapidated houses lined part of the journey raising a sorrowful thought in James' head. His first experience of the historic peninsula was to play a role in its destruction. Only months ago, those properties were filled with families getting on with their lives without harm to others. Where were those families now?

A shell exploded somewhere close by, and James was ripped violently from his thoughts. All the men fell to the ground, most in terror. It was the first encounter with deadly weapons for most men, but it would be far from the last.

Once they reached the trenches, the men were given a lecture on the dos and don'ts of their new accommodation: where to stand; what to listen out for; and how to sleep through the constant barrage of noise. They were also warned not to sit around moping and writing letters all day as that would guarantee frostbite or rheumatism. It was better for the mindset to keep physically active. The ones that did invariably outlived those that didn't.

Around them, soldiers leaned against the mud walls chatting amongst themselves and showing little interest in the latest recruits other than a few chuckles or shaking of heads. James studied the men in one small group. They looked to vary in age from years younger than him to older than his father. But the youngest, although perhaps not older than sixteen, had a weary expression far beyond his years.

Their temporary home was nowhere near as habitable as the ship which had delivered them to it. The aisles were sodden and stinking with rats that were running around more than the men. One new recruit joked that the rats were there first so the men should see themselves as the unwelcome animals. Another argued that rats didn't live under the soil like worms, and that the rodents would follow humans to Hell to make it more horrible. James listened to the two men who were spending their first few hours talking about anything but the war. They argued over the names of the stars in the night sky and which ball of light was Jupiter and which one was Venus. They guessed the first names of every soldier who walked by causing much amusement between them. When a stretcher was carried past, they did not comment and somehow ignored the screams coming from the wounded soldier lying on it. The unlucky man had stepped on a landmine. James and Douglas exchanged knowing glances.

Luck would indeed play a part in their experience of war.

***

Lilly sat alone in the small bleak whitewashed cell, her head down and hands clasped together as though in prayer. It was cold, but there were no goose pimples on her skin or hairs standing on end because the life had left her. Devoid of hope, her devastated heart had no strength to pump the blood around her body.

The only other person she had spoken to in the past twenty-four hours was the woman who'd brought her food and water and then collected the untouched tray the following hour.

'You might as well eat something, cos no one's gonna care if you don't,' the woman had said without a hint of compassion.

Not that the woman's mockery bothered Lilly. It was nothing compared to the grave judgements of those men in the court who'd viewed her as one of the worst kind of defendants — those accused of the crime of 'theft by a servant'. If that wasn't bad enough, Lilly had been a servant living in the relative splendour of a great mansion and was treated so kindly by Lord and Lady Fortesque who had provided her with the same education as their own daughters.

Her case was deemed too serious to deal with in the police court so she was being held in a cell until brought to trial. Lilly knew the Old Bailey judges could give the harshest of sentences — hard labour, transportation, and hanging. Of course, she would not be hanged as nobody had died. Also, women were not expected to break stones or cut logwood. Rather, prison life for a woman was filled with endless washing and ironing. It was servant work but without any pay. More like slavery.

Lilly's greatest fear was transportation, being sent to the new world from where no one ever returned. Those were the taunts that several prison workers had enjoyed inflicting on her from the moment that police constable had brought her in. They said she was the type of prisoner the camps abroad were crying out for as she was young and strong. The only reassuring words came from another female prisoner, a habitual offender, who told her not to listen to the cruel gibes as women were no longer deported. But Lilly found herself fearing the worst regardless.

She should have listened to Sam. He'd been horrified when she'd brought back the money from the pawnshop. Not that he blamed her for wanting to turn the traumatic experience she'd undergone into something positive. When she first discovered the necklace in her pocket, her immediate thought was to send it back to the Fortesques. She intended giving it to Adam as soon as she saw him. Arabella was always keen to travel to London. Lilly had even written a letter to include with the package she would give to Adam.

Yet time went by and there was no sign of the young driver. How she wished that fate had not caused her path to cross with the landlady the other morning. Then she would not have gone to that particular pawnshop, the one whose owner had insisted on taking her address before giving her the collection ticket. He must have already been informed about the missing necklace as within hours of her getting home, the police constable arrived.

The last time Lilly had seen Sam was at the police court and his angry expression caused her more worry. She knew he would do anything to free her which included confronting James Murdoch. If only she could talk to him, she would make him see reason. Even if James admitted everything, it would not change the fact that she had been caught trying to pawn jewellery that was not her own.

There was nothing he could do to help her, nothing anyone could do.

Chapter Fifteen

For Emily, it was a relief to be spending so much of the day with Tommy. Unlike her mother, he could not read every facial expression or recognise certain changes in tone. Rather, he was too wrapped up in his plans to analyse her behaviour. After John and Tommy had lifted the urn onto the attached cart, Tommy helped Emily onto the seat before joining her and taking the reins. Waving goodbye to her parents, Emily determined to block out all miserable thoughts for the whole day.

As they set off for Bamley Hall, Emily leant back against the urn and fixed her sore eyes on the horizon far ahead of them. It was going to be a long journey, but at least the land was flat thus the wheels would turn smoothly. Without realising, she closed her eyes and drifted into a half-sleep.

It was Tommy's hand grabbing her waistband that woke Emily up. She had been falling forward. After dragging her back against the urn, he pulled on the reins and stopped the horse and cart.

'Now, that's no way to sleep,' he laughed. 'You'll have a bad neck and be good for nothing by the time we get to Bamley Hall.'

Emily gasped with horror at the thought of what might have happened. 'Oh, Tommy, I'm sorry but I couldn't stop my eyes from closing. You see, I hardly slept last night.'

'No need for sorry. It's a long journey and there's little need for us both to be wide-eyed. Here!' He took off his coat and placed it on his lap. 'Rest your head on this so I can keep track of you.'

It was an outrageous suggestion, and her instinct was to decline, yet she knew he was right. Being so tired made her a danger to herself and risked the journey ending badly. And somehow, the coat looked like a very comfortable pillow. Without further thought, she said, 'Well, maybe for a few minutes, just to rest my eyes.'

The rhythmic turning of the wheels sent Emily into a light sleep short enough not to make her feel even worse. Opening her eyes after twenty minutes, she felt ready to face the next couple of hours. However, having a clear head made her more aware of how bedraggled she must look, in addition to the rather improper nature of her short sleep. With her head still resting on Tommy's coat, Emily wondered how she was going to sit up again. The easiest way would be to rest her hand on Tommy's leg but that was not a serious option. Before she had a chance to think of another, Tommy's large hand slipped under her arm and lifted her upright.

While brushing her face to hide her burning cheeks, she said, 'Oh, thank you. How did you know I was awake?'

'Your breathing changed,' he said, still looking ahead. The intimacy of his observation appeared to hit him as soon as he said it. His cheeks reddened too.

Neither traveller was able to find any further words to douse the heated atmosphere that had engulfed them. Instead, they continued in silence until reaching their destination at which point their unspoken relief was palpable.

At the end of the long driveway, Tommy guided the horse and cart around to the servants' entrance where a young, uniformed male was waiting. After helping Tommy carry the milk urn inside, the servant took the horse away for water and rest.

Emily and Tommy went into the kitchen where a nervous young maid gave them a slice of meat pie and some tea which Mrs Mallard had prepared. The cook wore a white apron tied tightly around her ample body, and her grey curls were tucked under a frilly white cap. Despite having the appearance of a warm-hearted grandmother, she scolded the maid with such ferocity that neither visitor could speak any words other than to thank her. Tommy widened his eyes at Emily who then nudged him under the table. Both had forgotten their recent awkwardness towards each other.

Having sent the maid away, Mrs Mallard focussed her attention on Tommy and Emily. 'Now you've got room in your cart, you can take that girl with you for nothing.'

Emily gave an embarrassed smile but Tommy's response surprised her.

'I suppose she must be new to be so unsure of herself?'

The cook snorted. 'Don't be fooled by incompetence. She's as new as that table you're eating off and lucky to still have a position here.'

'You must be a generous employer,' Tommy said. He did not mention that any generosity shown would be from the Lord and Lady of the house rather than their servants.

However, Mrs Mallard seemed to take the remark as a personal compliment. 'Well, people say I have the patience of a saint.'

'This is such a large residence I imagine there are many workers to take care of. Are you needing any staff, Mrs

Mallard? I have an uncle who may need a position later in the year.'

A surprised Emily shot a look at Tommy. 'Really! I didn't know that Tommy.'

'You don't know everything about me, Emmy,' he said, before turning back to the cook. 'My uncle is an experienced farmer but will consider anything that comes with lodging. He has a wife, you see, and she can put her hand to anything.'

'Now, if you'd come a week earlier, I could have helped you. One of our maids left a few weeks back, but her position has been filled.'

'But why did she want to leave here?' Tommy said in a tone of disbelief. 'Was it to marry?'

Mrs Mallard shook her head. 'I don't think that was the reason she left, though there was a young man in her life. They're unlikely to be getting married anytime soon though.'

'Why? Has something happened to her?'

After turning her head almost full circle to check no one else was around, Mrs Mallard sat on the chair next to Emily. 'The silly girl ran off with her mistress' jewellery, thought she would sell it no doubt. Now she's sleeping in a cold damp cell instead of the lovely room she had here.'

'And the mistress? How has she reacted?'

'She was upset to think that her most trusted maid was a common thief, but now she's forgotten all about it.'

'And she thinks Lil... the maid stole the jewellery?'

It was too late. The cook stared at Tommy and then stood up quickly. 'I'll take these now you've finished. Your horse will be readily refreshed by now.'

Outside, Emily could not wait to question Tommy. 'What were you up to in there? Why ask all those questions?'

Tommy shrugged. 'First I was fishing for possible work for your ma and pa. But after she mentioned Lilly, I got a bit distracted. I thought she might say something that would help Lilly... but I messed things up.'

Seeing Tommy's despondent look touched Emily's heart. She grabbed his arm. 'You are a good man, Tommy Barker, wanting to help my family and Lilly for no benefit to yourself. I'm proud of you for trying.'

She kissed him on the cheek.

***

Dawn was breaking and there was an uneasy quietness around the camp. James had yet to experience any fighting and felt almost as if he and Douglas were acting a part in a theatre play. However, later that evening the men were called to attention. Orders had been given for an offensive the following morning. There were ironic cheers from a couple of the seasoned soldiers. The recruits listened in silence. Despite having been in the siege line less than forty-eight hours, it was enough time for them to witness the condition of the wounded soldiers brought back from battle. One man had half his face blown off yet still managed to cry out in pain. Another was riddled with so many bloody holes he resembled a dummy used in the training camp. Already no one was under the illusion that what lay ahead for them was a gloriously clean combat of the kind they'd read about in story books. That dream had been left behind in the faraway hills of Great Britain.

It was a cold and dank morning and infantrymen were in a horizontal line behind the defensive redoubts they had built. The rain that had fallen persistently overnight had caused a thick mist which obscured the Russian fortifications ahead. The enemy could be feet away for all they knew.

Standing side by side, James and Douglas stared towards their unknown destiny. There was little point in being scared. Whatever fate awaited them, it would have little to do with their own actions. They were far more likely to be killed or injured by a shell than by an enemy bayonet. The previous evening, the friends had argued about which of them would likely die first. Both agreed it would be Douglas but for different reasons. James joked that Douglas, in his thirst for action, would advance so fast, he would leave his comrades far behind and be isolated. Whereas, Douglas insisted he would kill a dozen Russians before being struck by a wayward British shell. Now, the humour had gone from their talk.

'This is it, old bean,' Douglas said. 'Finally, we shall be battle-hardened heroes.'

'Yes,' James replied. 'We shall have much to discuss over lunch.'

'Absolutely. It will require another letter to Arabella before this one arrives.' Douglas patted his breast pocket. 'She must know of all the heroics of her fiancé.'

James sighed at the reference. 'I was drunk when I wrote that letter, Douglas. You can jolly well burn it when we return.'

'But why? You wrote it with such tenderness.'

'But I meant not a word of it, Douglas. Give it to me now.'

'I would need to unbutton my coat in order to do that.'

'Well. If I fall, do not send it.'

'If you fall, why should you care?'

Why should he care? James did not respond.

A bombardment began and the infantry waited for two hours until the commander gave a signal stirring them into action. Keeping low to the ground, the soldiers moved forward as various messages passed along them.

'Stay together. Save your bullets. Use your bayonets.'

Yet gunfire was everywhere.

James crawled along with his eyes fixed ahead and his mind still blocked from the sense of fear and dread trying to force its way inside. All around him, voices whispered or shouted commands but he could not hear the words clearly enough. Briefly, he turned to his right to see an older soldier was crawling where Douglas had been only seconds earlier. Was Douglas injured? James' heart wanted to go back and search for his friend; his head knew that would be pointless. Instead, he continued towards the enemy fire.

Someone cried out a warning. A sheet of flames was followed by an explosion that deafened all ears within fifty yards. The air was hissing with falling rocks and shell fragments. Above the cacophony of explosions, the command was given to run forward with muskets raised. James staggered into the blinding flashes of light and piercing whistling sounds which quickly became interspersed with men's screams and agonizing cries. He stumbled over and fell onto something soft, warm and wet. It was a soldier with half his body gone. As James was getting to his feet, he heard the sickening thud of a shell dropping close by. He heard nothing else.

***

Work at the farm was returning to normal, with Emily back at her dairy duties and Tommy being an effective replacement for Sam. The only worries were how Sam was coping in London, and whether he had found someone to defend Lilly in her upcoming trial. There had been no word since his brief visit the week before, which was a constant cause of worry for his mother. However, Tommy assured them his contact in London would do as much as he could to help Sam and Lilly. The reason for his confidence was made clear. On one voyage, several sailors had tried to persuade others to take control of the ship. They planned to direct it to a country where they could find refuge in return for some of the gold the ship was carrying. Loyal to his employers, Tommy informed the captain. Between them, they managed to overcome the would-be mutineers. Of course, the shipowner was incredibly grateful and said they should come to him if ever they needed help.

Emily listened in awe at the tale of swashbuckling bravery trying to imagine Tommy grappling with those bad men on the deck of a ship. She dared not ask if they were forced to walk the plank. John and Mara, slightly more sceptical, wondered to what extent Tommy had exaggerated his heroics. They were impressed, nonetheless.

'We cannot thank you enough for your trouble, lad,' John said, 'but a shipowner cannot defend Lilly in court.'

'He is a man of great standing and is sure to know a solicitor or two.'

'But even if he finds Lilly a solicitor, how can they afford to pay him?' Mara said. Not expecting an answer to her question, she began to clear the table.

'Some are more costly than others, but perhaps he will pay the fee himself,' Tommy said, though without the confident tone of earlier.

'A rich man does not give his money away,' John said mockingly. 'He had plenty of opportunity to reward you at the time.'

On hearing her father's words, Emily cringed. Poor Tommy didn't deserve such a scornful response to his offer of help. Hoping to move the subject on, she said, 'Perhaps we should go to the trial to show our support and keep Sam company. They must feel so wretched.'

Nobody responded. It was a ridiculous suggestion as the farm could barely afford to lose one worker let alone the whole family. They had managed Emily's illness and Sam's departure but not without a struggle. The last thing they needed was another upheaval just when all had settled. An unexpected knock on the door was about to shatter that relative stability.

Another knock, louder that time. Emily's father stood up and walked to the door, steadying himself before he opened it. He was faced by Michael Tiggs, a local toolmaker who had climbed back into his wagon. Tiggs called for Tommy to come outside. John returned to the kitchen.

Less than a minute passed before Tommy came in from outside. His face was taut and his eyes distant signalled that his mind was elsewhere.

'There has been an accident in the stable. A horse kicked my father in the head and he is very poorly. Forgive me, but I must go to him immediately.'

Bowing his head towards the table, he rushed back outside leaving the Mayers in stunned silence.

At last, Emily found her tongue. 'Poor Mr Barker. I hope he will be alright.'

John Mayer, pessimistic by nature, shook his head. A kick from a horse is as good as a bullet from a gun. We will not see Arnie Barker again.'

Mara scolded her husband for his unsparing language. 'There is no need for such talk,' she said, shifting her eyes towards their daughter. 'For the moment, we know nothing more than he is hurt so let us wait until we hear more.'

However, it seemed that John had made up his mind already. 'I swear this farm is meant to go to nothing. We might as well all pack in our tools and go to the workhouse already.'

Emily and her mother exchanged glances knowing there was no point in challenging John when he was at his most dejected. Instead, Mara focused on the Barkers' misfortune and what they could do to help out. It was agreed that she and her husband would visit the Barker family the following day. Emily would take care of the dairy.

Chapter Sixteen

Lilly sat with her head to the side, unable to look at the twelve faces opposite the dock. Instead, she fixed her eyes on the blond head she could just about make out in the public gallery. Between them sat several men wearing black gowns and wigs. One of those men was meant to be on her side but she could not tell one from the other. After all, since arriving at the court everything had been a whirlwind. Men and women were brought in and then taken out again. Some were grim-faced and in chains. Some smiled with loved ones. Some were expressionless. With the speed of the hearings, Lilly realised she was a number, not a person. Her life did not matter to the men in wigs and black gowns who appeared to be joking with each other while waiting for the drama to begin.

What chance did she have?

A harsh voice ordered everyone to rise from their seats allowing Lilly to catch sight of Sam for the first time. Their eyes met and he gave a meek smile which she desperately wanted to return but knew it would be frowned upon by the jury. Into the courtroom came the judge, also wearing a black gown, but his wig was longer than the other men of law. An exhausted Lilly struggled to stand and almost fell back down before permission had been given to sit. A burly officer grabbed and held her upright, squeezing her arm so tightly that she had to stop herself from crying out. It was a relief to finally sit down despite it signalling the start of the trial.

A second harsh male voice called out:

Lillian Bexley is accused of stealing one diamond-encrusted gold pendant and one gold chain, the goods of Arabella Fortesque, her mistress, in her dwelling.

For the first time, the attention of the entire courtroom fell on the dock. Lilly began to shake uncontrollably. Out of nowhere, a familiar-looking man dressed in a tweed suit appeared. He walked into the witness stand, taking with him the eyes of everyone, including Lilly.

One of the wigged gentlemen asked him his name and occupation.

'William Arthur Golding. I own Golding Goldsmith & Silversmith in Andover Street, London.'

Of course. It was the man from the pawnshop. The court listened as he gave his evidence:

I keep a jewellery shop in Andover Street, in the parish of Lambeth; the prisoner came into my shop on 20th September, the last thing before the close of day. She placed a valuable gold necklace in my hands. I saw that the item was expensive but said I could only offer a pound. That was on condition I saw proof of address. The prisoner accepted and offered her rent book which I examined. Later that day, Police Constable Morris showed me a list of stolen items. I immediately recognized the necklace.

Staring at the old man sitting in the witness stand, Lilly thought what a terrible judge of character she must have been. After entering the shop, her first impression of Mr Golding was that he would sell his soul to the devil for a few shillings. Yet he was honest enough to show the necklace to the policeman despite having paid out some of his own money as a deposit. No. It was Lilly who was dishonest. That was why she was the one sitting in the dock. As if to add salt to her wounds, the jeweller was asked to identify the person about whom he'd been speaking. He pointed at Lilly causing an exaggerated hush from the public gallery.

The next witness was the landlady who kept describing herself as an honest woman, distraught at the realisation she had given refuge to a common thief. To Lilly's eyes, the whole courtroom agreed, possibly even Sam. Then a wigged man who had been sitting quietly, got out of his seat and marched up to Mrs Murphy. His clipped accent was posher than Lord Fortesque's.

"You are aware of the reward for the necklace, are you not?" the barrister said.

"Er, well, I wasn't until —'

"You found out from Mr Golding, did you not?'

"Yeah, but —'

'And it was you who persuaded the defendant to visit Mr Golding when she had given no prior thought to the possibility of selling the necklace.'

Rather than continuing to argue, Mrs Murphy folded her arms and, after muttering "yes", fell silent.

In terms of the case as a whole, it was a small victory but at least Lilly was reminded of her good intentions. Then, she was called to give her own explanation as to how she came to have the necklace in her possession. In a trembling voice she said:

After Miss Arabella left her room, I saw the pendant on the floor. I knew the chain was certain to be there too, so I knelt down to see if I could feel it on the carpet. I found the chain and put it in my pocket and then the candle went out. A man grabbed me and tried to force himself on me but I managed to get away. The next morning, I was frightened and angry and in a panic in case I came across him again. I decided to leave but in my haste forgot I still had the necklace.

On being asked why she didn't inform her employers of the incident, Lilly replied that the attacker was one of the guests.

"The candle was extinguished therefore how could you be certain that it was not a male servant?"

"He did not sound like a servant and he smelt badly of alcohol. Also, I tore part of his jacket. I saw him leaving the following morning with that same jacket."

"Do you know the name of that man?"

"Yes, I do. It was James Murdoch."

There were gasps of shock from the public gallery at such an outrageous accusation. Although most did not know who the named man was, it was clear that he was a gentleman. Lilly even noticed a flash of doubt in the eyes of her barrister. Or had she imagined it? In that moment of despondency, Lilly's eyes searched for Sam among the hordes of unknown faces. There was only one person she recognised but it was not him.

It was Arabella.

***

After her parents left for the Barkers, Emily began her milking duties. A short while later, having finished the morning milking, she began to break up the small amount of curd. It was a mindless act requiring little concentration and her mind began to wander.

She realised it was the first time she'd been properly alone since her encounter with James. She hadn't even been to the meadow as her foot was not yet healed enough to make the short journey. Or was it that she could not face the thought of being there without a chance of him joining her? But then why would he? She had given him all of herself and had no more to offer. He was going to marry Arabella who would be wearing a white dress, something Emily would never be able to do with all honesty.

A solitary tear trickled down her cheek and dropped into the thickening mixture. Disgusted with herself, she rubbed her fingers clean and moved away before she could do further damage. Then the tears rolled too fast to stem. Folding her arms around her head, she allowed herself to wallow in self-pity.

The sound of a horse stopping outside the dairy was unfamiliar. Emily's heart almost jumped through her chest.

Was it him? Had he returned from Scotland to explain that it had all been a terrible mistake? With bated breath, she listened as the rider dismounted the neighing horse. The footsteps got nearer and nearer. Panicked, she wiped the tears away from her sodden cheeks. She was facing the door when the footsteps stopped.

Tommy walked into the dairy without saying a word. He stood just inside the door. Although brief, the silence between them was unusual. The air was tense.

Emily forced herself to speak first.

'Tommy! What are you doing here? Your family need you.'

Still not speaking, Tommy merely shook his head in a response that made no sense to Emily. She stepped forward and noticed the sadness in his grey eyes. 'Oh no. Please don't tell me ...'

At last, Tommy said, 'The injury was severe. My father could not be saved.'

Emily cried. 'Oh, Tommy, that is terrible. I don't know what to say.' She stepped forward and touched his arm gently. 'I have almost finished here. Once the cows are back, let us go inside and I'll make some tea.'

Tommy took the animals back to their small field while Emily went on inside to prepare the tea. Ten minutes later, both were sitting opposite each other with an untouched steaming teapot in front of them. Once again, Emily was the one who directed the conversation.

'What is your poor mother going to do? I cannot imagine how distraught she must be ... and having to worry about the business as well with you going ...'

He picked up his empty cup and rubbed his finger down a fine crack in the china. 'I cannot go now. I'll need to take over the forge if my mother is to stay at the house.'

'But how can you do that? Your father is ... was a skilled blacksmith.'

'And I helped him before leaving home. I know the ins and outs of shoeing a horse more than anyone else around these parts.'

'But your plans, Tommy. You are meant to sail soon.'

'Things happen and plans change. My mother is in need, and I must do what I can to help. I only feel bad for your family. It means I can no longer help out here.'

'Oh, don't.' She leaned over the table and took both of his hands in hers. 'You have helped us all you can. Your duty is with your own family now.' A flash of emotion showed in his eyes and Emily knew it was pain. 'Has my father tried to persuade you to stay here even longer? You must not listen to him. And it is the same with your own family. I know how much you have been looking forward to July and beginning the next voyage. It is enough that you gave up the last one. Your life is your own to live and you must go with your heart.'

Again Tommy shook his head. 'Much has happened since then, not just Sam leaving and my father's accident, but more.'

'What else is there?' she asked.

He gently released his hands from hers and got to his feet. 'There is you, Emmy. You tell me to go with my heart, but my heart would break without you.'

Emily's eyes widened and her mouth dropped open. Now, she was the one to shake her head. 'I did not know. You showed no signs.'

'I know you can't love me, Emmy, but if you let me take care of you, I will love you forever. Will you marry me, Emmy?'

Emily stared at the man she had only come to know recently. He was unlike James in so many ways - fair hair, grey eyes, bronzed skin rough and scarred from manual labour. And the differences went beneath the skin. While James was selfish and impetuous, Tommy was loyal to his family and eager to do the right thing. He was a better man than James. But he was right; she didn't love him. However, it was not the time to cause him further pain.

'This has taken me by surprise and I have had no time to consider my own feelings for you.'

A glint of hope showed in his eyes and he approached her. Kneeling, he grasped her hands in his. ‘For you to consider marrying me is enough. I will allow you all the time you need.’

Chapter Seventeen

The grey stone walls seemed to be closing in on Lilly as she stood in the centre of the cell waiting to hear her fate. She no longer feared transportation, particularly as the jury had recommended mercy. At least they believed her story. Besides, it was rare for a woman to still be deported, even if there was external pressure. Lilly was confident the Fortesques would not choose to use their influence in such a vindictive way. In fact, Arabella's face had paled when the guilty verdict was read out even though it had not been a shock to anyone else in the courtroom, Lilly included. After all, she had taken the necklace. That it was an accident mattered not once she had gone on to pawn it. She had known it was not hers to sell. How could the verdict have been anything else?

Her eyes had fixed on Arabella to avoid looking at Sam. She could not bear to have his devastated face as her last memory of him if, as one of the prison guards suggested, she was denied visitors.

After two hours of solitude, Lilly could stand no longer and sat on the wooden slats fixed into the wall. Being closer to the stone floor, she became aware of the unpleasant odours coming from it — urine, vomit, blood. She wanted to scream out loud to remind those outside that she was still there. Instead, she remained still and silent and listened to the various sounds outside the heavy metal door: the heavy footsteps of guards coming and going; doors opening and closing; and voices sounding and fading away. Yet no one bothered to peer through the small hatch to see if she was still alive.

Despite the cold air, Lilly closed her eyes and forced her mind to another place. She was sitting in the kitchen of Bamley Hall. Adam was next to her. They were both crying. Mrs Mallard snapped at them before giving them apple pie and custard. It was Lilly's first day away from home but Adam had come from the workhouse. Lilly had forgotten that she'd cried. Or had she? Whether a memory or a dream, she was jolted out of the vision by the heavy clanking of the door. Having no idea how long had passed since she'd first sat down, her mind was in a state of confusion. That was about to intensify when the door finally opened.

Arabella was standing a few feet away. Her face was as pale as milk, her eyes glazed and lifeless and her hair hidden under a white fur hat. Looking so beautiful, she might have been a statue or an angel. Lilly could only stare in wonder. Neither woman spoke and the surreal experience continued until a police officer came in and broke the spell. After placing a chair in the centre of the floor, he left the cell.

Arabella spoke quietly.

'This has all come as a terrible shock to us, Lilly. What were you thinking?'

Hearing the judgemental tone of her former mistress, Lilly's eyes filled with tears of anger and misery. She wanted to ask Arabella what right she thought she had to add to her punishment It was fortunate she was unable to summon up the strength to speak.

Arabella sat down on the wooden chair and folded both hands on her lap. 'I wish you had come to me, Lilly. It was most improper of you to leave without a word ... not even to Mrs Mallard who was very distressed.'

At the mention of Mrs Mallard, Lilly suddenly felt a smattering of guilt. The cook could be bad-tempered, but she'd looked after the younger servants as if they were her own family.

'I'm sorry, Miss, but I was not thinking properly. When I saw him standing there with you, and your fondness for him, I thought it better that I left without explanation. It would only have upset you further.'

'But Lilly, you are mistaken. It was not James who tried to force himself on you, whatever that means.'

'Pardon me, Miss, but I know what I saw,' Lilly said.

'No, Lilly. You think you know what you saw. You yourself said that the candle was extinguished. It would not have been possible to see the man's face or even his clothes. How can you be so confident he was not a servant? Many times I have smelt ale on Adam when he is driving me back from London. Are you certain it was not him? There were any number of men it might have been. It is unfair of you to accuse a man who is unable to defend himself.'

All that Lilly could interpret from the jumble of words was that Arabella was trying to defend James Murdoch. That was why she was sitting in a squalid cell and talking to a convicted criminal. It was not for Lilly's sake that she was demeaning herself. But the reason Lilly was in that cell was that she was attacked by James Murdoch. The last thing she was going to do was lie to clear his name.

'Begging your pardon, Miss, but I saw enough to be certain. I may not have seen his face but I felt his height and heard his voice. Also, I am well aware of the difference in quality between the jackets of a gentleman and a servant. And, as I told the court, in the struggle I ripped the breast pocket of his jacket. I saw him with that same jacket the following morning.'

On hearing Lilly's account, Arabella sighed. 'The jacket did not belong to James. He had been ill during the evening and soiled his own jacket. Because he was leaving early the following morning, he borrowed his friend's. Although ripped, it was still clean.'

Lilly frowned. Was Arabella lying to protect the man she loved? If not, she would be in even more trouble for defaming an innocent man. Her solicitor had warned her of the risk. He even implied it would be better to admit to stealing the necklace rather than upset a rich and powerful family. But Lilly was proud and not willing to pretend her assault was not the cause of her current misfortune. She wanted to punish the man who attacked her.

'Who was his friend?'

'That matters not,' Arabella replied quickly. 'And it could only bring you more trouble to know.'

'How could I be in more trouble? I am waiting to hear how long I shall spend in prison for theft because of his friend.'

Arabella raised her eyebrows at the uncharacteristic tone of her former maid. Shaking her head, she stood up and walked towards the door. Suddenly, she stopped. 'Oh yes. Silly me. I almost forgot. Papa has spoken to the judge. They have agreed that in lieu of a prison sentence, you are to return to Balham Hall for two years without pay. So, no, Lilly, you will not go to prison. Please be thankful for the mercy you have been shown.'

Lilly tried to digest the last few sentences. Those sentences bore little relation to what had been discussed since Arabella first entered the cell. 'I do not understand what you are saying, Miss. What does all that mean?'

'You must return to Balham Hall, Lilly. At once.'

***

As Emily was walking down the stairs, she heard her mother singing and immediately knew something had changed for the better. She couldn't imagine it had anything to do with Tommy as there was no bringing his poor father back from the grave. Nor would Tommy have said anything about his proposal of marriage. He said he did not want to pressure Emily further and she believed him. No. It could only be related to one person.

'Morning, Ma. You are washing already. Did you not sleep well?'

Mara turned her head while continuing to wring out a sheet over the doorstep. Her eyes were glistening but not from tears.

'I slept not an hour, Emily, because there is so much to do before he comes home.'

Emily gasped. 'What has happened? Has he left poor Lilly?'

'Don't you go worrying yourself over that girl. She's brought on her own misfortune.'

'But surely you cannot say she deserves to go to prison, not when she was, well, after what she said.' Emily could not bring herself to repeat Lilly's claim as hearing it once had nearly destroyed her will to live.

Mara disappeared outside to hang up the sheet before returning to make breakfast. She was no longer singing but her lips were in a fixed smile.

'Lilly is no more going to prison than I am to the moon. She's been given a second chance and is returning to her position with the Fortesques.'

'What! But why ever would she agree to that? She was desperate to live in London and hated being a maid.'

'It was not for her to agree to anything. The only choice she had was Balham Hall or prison. Not even Lilly is daft enough to consider a filthy cell in Newgate a price worth paying to live in London.'

'But she would be living in the same place, and he ...'

Mara stopped buttering the bread slice in her hand. 'And what, luv?'

'He'll be there,' she blurted out, before bursting into uncontrollable sobs.

Placing the bread and knife on the table, Mara wiped her greasy hands and sat in the opposite chair. Then, taking her daughter's hands in hers, she spoke softly.

'Emily, luv, there is something you should know and it will upset you greatly.' The glowing smile had disappeared from her face.

Looking up, Emily stared into her mother's eyes suspiciously. She braced herself for the news that James and Arabella were already married. What she was about to hear was far worse.

'Yesterday, news came through that James Murdoch was killed during a battle. I am sorry, luv.'

Emily's mouth dropped open and her eyes crinkled in confusion. 'What battle? He is only training.'

'A battle in Russia.'

Russia. Battle. Killed. Emily did not allow herself to be upset because what her mother was saying made no sense. 'Ma, you are mistaken,' she whispered, snatching her hands away. 'James is in Scotland. I know because he told me. He will be returning any day now.'

Mara shook her head. 'He joined as a volunteer but probably got carried away with all the hullaballoo in the newspapers. The battle was two days ago. It was his first. Those poor, stupid young men are trained to think there is honour and glory in killing others. I truly regret his death but he was a fool, and you are better off without him.'

With her head pounding with the horrific news, Emily had one last hope. 'If he died two days ago, how could you know already? It makes no sense to me.'

'It makes little sense to me either but it is said that they have built a telegraph cable reaching the battlegrounds. The newspapers know everything within the day. It is a terrible, pointless war and those responsible for it deserve to be punished. Here's your father so best not say anything more.'

But Emily was no longer listening. Without saying another word, she rose from her seat and left the house. There was only one place she wanted to be.

***

The green landscape was a sight for Sam's sore eyes as his train weaved through the countryside. How he had missed those fields, hills and trees covering so much of the land; how he wanted to breathe in that fresh air. He and Lilly hadn't been confined to a square mile of concrete and dust for as long as all that. Yet to Sam, it had seemed like years. The last month had been a waking nightmare from which he could see no escape. However, thanks to the Fortesques, the nightmare was over.

Despite knowing Lilly would be found guilty, Sam longed for the end of the trial to begin making plans to be as close to her as possible. He'd even asked Tommy about the possibility of working in Australia in case she was deported.

Yet rather than moving to the other side of the world, he and Lilly were going backwards to where they had spent much or most of their lives. It would be as though the past couple of months had never happened. Well, not exactly.

Although happy to take Lilly back, the Fortesques had not extended their trust as far as allowing her to retake her position. Rather, she was to be kept in the kitchen to do the work of a scullery maid, besides any other duties that Mrs Mallard could find for her. Apart from washing and sleeping, Lilly would not be allowed to leave the kitchen for one whole year. For the following year, she would need the Fortesques' permission. She would not even have a wage, only her board and lodge. At first, Sam wondered if there was much difference between that sentence and the alternative. Would she even be safe in the house where her attacker visited so often? But the news of James Murdoch's death removed that concern.

For Sam, next to nothing would change. He would be back living with his parents in the house where he was born and doing the same work since leaving school. Of course, there were slight differences. Lilly would no longer be able to visit him at the farm. That would mean extra journeys to Balham Hall. It was a small price to pay to be able to hold her in his arms again. They had not spoken since before the trial, and he could not wait to give her his shoulder to cry on. He would wipe away all her tears.

***

Emily didn't stop running until she reached the spot she knew so well. The meadow had changed almost beyond recognition since she had been there last. A blanket of multicoloured leaves covered the short grass and the bare trees held on the decaying nests in their branches. Emily imagined the new life that had fledged within those homes so expertly woven from twigs and grass. Those fluffy little birds that lined the branches while watching their parents demonstrate how to fly were now far away. In the distance, several groups of starlings were weaving patterns in the sky before merging into one. At that moment, Emily would have given her life to fly away with them.

Seconds later, a blackbird flew onto a low branch above the hollow and began to sing. Emily took out the bread she'd slipped into her pocket while her mother wasn't looking. Tearing off pieces, she tossed them onto the grass. The female blackbird appeared joining the male on the branch, but neither left their perch. Slowly Emily stepped forward. Still, the birds did not move. Another step. Then another. If she raised her arms, she could almost touch them.

As she stared back at the two blackbirds, she thought how different they looked. To an amateur birdwatcher, they could be different species: the handsome male with his glossy black plumage, bright orange-yellow beak, and yellow eye rings, his famous melodic song recognised by all, next to the dowdy, brown-feathered female with her indistinguishable chirps. But there was no other mate for the majestic male.

'Only humans judge you,' Emily said, looking at the female.

Perhaps because her voice startled them, the birds flew off and resettled on a higher branch. Emily stared at the vacated branch and then at the hollow where she had left so much food in the past. There would be nothing remaining because she had not been back since that night. She put her hand into the dark space and felt inside — soggy leaves, twigs and something not created by nature. Pulling out the small box, she opened the lid to find a ring with a tiny sapphire in the centre. She threaded her finger through the gold band and held it to her cheek. Closing her eyes, she imagined he was there too. For a moment, a rush of sensations — his scent, taste and touch — swept the heartbreak from her body. The memories laid dormant within her and she hoped to always have them.

She took off the ring, placed it in her pocket, and went home.

Chapter Eighteen

The late autumn sun caused the spire to shine like the northern star. Yet the rays could not warm the half dozen people inside the small village church. Only the front pews were occupied. The marriage was by common licence and neither bride nor groom wanted guests beyond their immediate families. On one side of the aisle sat the male members of the Mayer family, John and Sam. Mara and Emily had yet to arrive. Opposite sat Mrs Barker and a girl of about fifteen, a niece who'd come to stay. At the end of their row, his face as white as a sheet sat a nervous Tommy.

Upstairs in the farmhouse, Emily stared at her reflection in the long mirror in her parent's bedroom. Her hair was newly curled and pinned with silk ribbons and miniature pink roses. The dress was beautiful especially considering Mrs Weekes had had less than a fortnight's notice to make it. The satin sleeves hugged her lean arms like skin, the skirt flowed out like leaves and the bodice pushed up her small breasts like buds in springtime. It was almost perfect.

Emily raised her hand to the neckline which was decorated with fabric flowers. All were white except for two. She felt the damp stain which marred the whiteness of the dress. Tears began to roll down her face leaving a trail of white through the rouged cheeks.

She felt two hands around her waist and her mother's face appeared in the mirror above her shoulder.

'I'll get some soap,' she said, before leaving the bedroom.

Shocked, Emily followed her mother downstairs. 'But, Ma, it would be wrong.'

'What would be wrong?' Mara said. 'We won't have time to dry it but it'll have to do.' She rubbed soap onto a wet cloth.

'It would be unfair on Tommy.'

'Don't worry about Tommy. He will be just fine. That man loves you. I see it every time he looks at you.'

'But —'

'But never mind. What he doesn't know won't hurt him. Now bring yourself over here.'

'It will come too soon.'

'No. The first is always late.'

'I would not be able to live with the guilt.'

Suddenly, Mara grabbed her daughter by the shoulders and shook her violently. 'The only thing you have to worry about is that,' she said. Her eyes falling on Emily's stomach. 'As for the guilt, you will just have to live with it.'

The sound of the hired cabriolet pulling up outside caused both women to look at the door anxiously and then back at each other.

'We'll be a few minutes, 'Mara shouted, before lowering her voice again. 'This will never be talked about again.'

***

Mara had prepared a small celebratory feast at the farmhouse where the handful of guests assembled to wish the newlyweds the best. A room in a small riverside hotel was booked for the honeymoon. It was only for one night as Tommy could not afford to be away from the family business for even a few days. The journey would take a couple of hours so they were due to leave before sunset. However, seeing Tommy and Sam enjoying the drink a bit too much, Mara packed the couple off mid-afternoon with enough food to see them through the rest of the day.

As their cabriolet was leaving Flemsbury, Emily took one last look at the meadow. She knew it would be a long time before she could return there. Perhaps never. The memories would be too intense to bear.

They were going to live with Mrs Barker. She had moved into the smaller bedroom leaving the larger one for the new couple. Emily knew the kind woman's eyes would be watching her constantly. She would never suspect anything of her new daughter. Nor would Tommy. Yet Emily would know and she could only hope that the child she was carrying would arrive late, as her mother had claimed. Not only that but it should resemble her, with fair hair not dark and eyes blue not black as coal.

A gentle kiss on the cheek woke Emily from her thoughts. She turned to Tommy and smiled. There were no tingles or shivers, only a warm tenderness. It was as though they had been a couple for ever.

Maybe fate had merely added a few bends in the path that would always bring them together. Or did either of them have a choice in their destination? The woman in the fair had thought so.

Emily would never know.

Epilogue

In the centre of a large open room in Constantinople, a small group of women stood together talking. Wearing identical clothes, a long black dress and a white cap, the women were only distinguishable by their faces. All were ignoring the cries of pain and anguish coming from the rows of narrow beds against the thick stone walls. Besides the occupied beds, bloodied and bandaged men lay out on the badly stained floorboards. A draft was coming in from the ugly broken windows, which caused a constant flickering of the candle placed on a dark wooden box in one corner.

Furthest away in the opposite corner, a single bed had been placed behind a pillar. The positioning of the bed was not to give the occupant some privacy, however. Rather, that particular spot was the darkest part of the room.

One of the women pulled a chair next to the bed. She pushed back a clump of blonde hair which had fallen from the cap. Then, in a firm but gentle voice said, 'You have a visitor.'

There was no visible response from the figure sitting on the bed as a thick woollen coat covered his head and upper body. It may have been that he did not hear the footsteps approaching him or the chair creaking from the weight of his visitor.

'The doctor said that you do not have any injuries so that is a blessing. Look, I cannot talk to you this way.' Turning to the doctors, he shouted, 'Someone remove this damned thing from his head.'

A doctor came over and spoke quietly to the visitor. 'Your son is suffering from temporary madness. He will recover quicker at home.'

'What sort of madness? He has a fiancée.'

'Perhaps you should mention her name. It may help.'

Leaning forward, the man said, 'Son, you must pull yourself together as your fiancée waits for you at home. Well, could someone take that thing away? I do not wish to shout out our business.'

The doctor waved to the young blonde nurse and pointed to the coat. She came over and gently lifted the heavy garment from the patient's head. Tentatively, she waited to see the effect of her action.

James' dark eyes did not react to the changed light nor did he appear to notice his father sitting mere inches away. Slowly his eyes turned to the nurse still holding the coat. He lifted his hand towards her and with his eyes, pleaded for her to come to him.

The nurse looked at the doctor. He nodded. With caution, she moved back to the bed and sat down next to James. Then she took his hand in hers.

'Can you hear me?' she said softly. 'James, please say something.'

'I've missed you,' he said.' He began to cry.

Printed in Dunstable, United Kingdom

77061089R00143